The heart that touched Heaven: The Virgin Mary and you

Dedication:

To John and Mary together with their children

Index

Introduction

After midnight, the usual silence of the neighborhood was broken by the intermittent flash of colored lights. Blue, red, white. The police siren cut through the cold air, and neighbors, awakened from their lethargy, began to peer out of windows and doors. Some, still in their pajamas, murmured among themselves as the scene unfolded like a movie no one expected to see. In the center of the street, two figures stood out amid the chaos. One, a tall, thin man, his face illuminated by the screen of his phone, seemed to have been waiting for something… or someone. The other, younger, was sweating under the weight of a bicycle that now lay on the ground, a silent witness to the incident.

"What's wrong with you?!" the cyclist shouted, his voice filled with fury. "You shouldn't have gotten in my way!" The other, calmer but visibly annoyed, raised an eyebrow and replied with sharp irony:

—Relax, champ. If you can't stop, it's not my fault.

Suddenly, everything escalated. A push, a brusque response, and the small spark became a fire. The neighbors, paralyzed between morbidity and prudence, watched the scene as if it were an improvised show. But what no one knew, what not even the protagonists of the fight could imagine, was that that night, on that street, their lives and those of those around them were about to change forever. Would the fight be a simple anecdote? Or the beginning of something bigger, something that would reveal the cracks, the secrets and the broken dreams of a neighborhood that seemed so peaceful from the outside? "One of them was called Little-I-care, and the other's name was What-will-they-say"[1]. What-will-they-say is knocked down by Little-I-care and falls to the ground. He is ashamed, he swears that he will get revenge. He says: this cannot be left like this, what will the girlfriend say. He gets up What-will-they-say and throws a strong blow to Little-I-care's face, knocks him down and his nose starts to bleed. Little-I-care gets up, wipes his face and notices that there is a small wooden stick within reach, he grabs it and starts hitting What-will-they-say with all his strength. The girlfriend is scared, she screamed, cried and tried to calm the situation but without any success. Both were furious. Little-I-care said that he did not care about going to jail, that they should call the police. What-will-they-say, inside, wanted to stop

---

[1] R. Llull, Felix or the Book of Marvels. Madrid, BAC, 2016. p. 218.

the fight but it was too late, besides, if he stopped fighting what would people and his girlfriend who was watching him say. Seeing the seriousness of the situation, a third person named Rigoroso appears, stating that the law must be applied. He quotes a phrase from the Bible to strengthen his argument: "Jesus said I have not come to abolish the law but to give it fullness," therefore, a situation like this cannot occur in a peaceful and working-class neighborhood, especially when people are resting. He warns them of the legal consequences that both were incurring; they argue heatedly, insult each other, lose control… more and more people join in, almost all the windows of the houses were full of curious observers, some recording with cell phones all the scenes that could be captured, others calling God knows who on the phone. The noise was increasing, many curious people appeared, some approached the scene of the events, others looked timidly from afar… in this context a YouTuber named Fructuoso appears. He warns them that he has been recording the entire scene from the beginning. He suggests that it is best for each one to recognize the wrong they have done, come to an agreement and end the fight. He also reminds them of a quote from the Gospel: "come to an agreement with your adversary, lest he hand you over to the bailiff and he hand you over to the judge and the judge put you in jail." What-do-I-care intervenes in an aggressive and hurtful manner, saying: What do you care! Don't meddle in other people's affairs! They confront each other heatedly. What-will-they-say enters the debate and says, if you have the recording, show me! Just in case it is just a story. What could people say on social media? I am a good believer, I go to church every week. I don't want to appear as a coward or a timid person. In any case, if you have recorded them, you are going to publish it or at least put us on your channel as two intransigent people. What do I care, he says, how little courage! Let him do what he wants! Here we are the problem. All these "peeping toms", a bunch of gossips who can go back to sleep, they have to work tomorrow, they seem to be having fun watching us argue. I am a volunteer at the Church but it doesn't matter what they say. The neighbors started shouting, they insulted, they cursed but they didn't show their faces.Many left but many others stayed waiting for the outcome. What-will-they-say suffered a lot because he felt he was the centre of attention. He felt discredited, he didn't even have the face to look at his girlfriend who wouldn't stop crying or complaining about why he had gotten into trouble. Neither of them wanted to give in, neither What-I-care nor What-will-they-say, one because he really didn't care at all, the other because he wanted to save face until the police finally arrived. They appeared making a horrible noise very typical of them together with another car that didn't have any police signs, but it was. They looked more like detectives. Two tall, dark-skinned policemen got out and immediately intervened, without investigating too much about what had happened they put the four of them in the police car: What-will-they-say, What-I-care, Rigorous and Fructuoso. The neighbours were scared, some murmured and said what a shame that they took away those who had nothing to do with it. They stood there doing nothing, many of those who were watching hid so as not to show their faces or explain anything, they were only interested in satisfying their curiosity and having a topic of conversation with their family or at work.

A tiny event has created a huge problem. An unexpected, private, but social event. It involved people who had nothing to do with the problem. This is how we live. Scholars claim that we are experiencing a social decline that is mainly expressed in each person choosing their own way of life, that is, we live in an era of the "me generation."[2]. Everything

---

[2]C. Taylor, The Ethics of Authenticity, London, Oxford University Press, 1994, p. 37-42.

is reduced to the subject, he becomes an end in himself and without any other purpose than his self. He tries to put everything under his control, he has lost the perspective that everything is in God's hands. If he has forgotten that everything is in God's hands then everything is in anyone's hands. The subject has become a slave to himself. He has lost his own freedom. What will they say has as its goal to keep up appearances, protect himself and maintain an image of himself that he has created over the years; What do I care, has as its goal to do whatever he wants, he cares about nothing but his own whim. Rigorous has as its goal the fulfillment of the law. Something very noble but insufficient to stop a small conflict. The law helps but does not make us friends and much less brothers. Fructuoso appeals to the facts and has noble goals, to fix the difficulties without going any further, however, he fails to offer a solution that convinces the characters in question. What do all these characters need to be able to stop the violence and avoid bigger problems? All four characters were believers, at least. Not all of them practice, but they recognize that God exists, even if they don't consider him at all. Let's say that all four have faith in their own way, but their faith is far from reason. Their life is led not by reason but by whim (What-do-I-care), appearance (What-will-they-say), law (Rigorous) and tranquility (Fructuous).

Something is needed that combines three dimensions: faith, reason and life. A marginal Jew called Jesus of Nazareth, among so many accurate statements that he makes, has one that could help us to continue to delve deeper: "He who is faithful in a little is faithful in much" (Luke 16, 10-13). It doesn't seem complicated to assume this idea, but who has lived this "ideal"? Is there anyone who has been able to practice what Jesus says? Without a doubt, the first person who lived these words very well was the Virgin Mary. When we think of her, many questions come to mind, such as: how did she live as a neighbor in Nazareth and in Egypt? How did she deal with the discussions that her son Jesus had with his adversaries? How did she deal with the death of her husband Joseph? etc. The gospels answer us clearly. She lived her life from faith and reason. In her we find a synthesis in the incarnation of faith, reason and life based on the concreteness of her life. In the little things, in her daily responsibilities, she embodied faith and reason. In her life we observe the synthesis of faith and reason. Faith and reason must be expressed in daily life; in small responsibilities. Putting the dialogue of faith and reason into practice in daily life. In the great academic debates it is not difficult to see the synthesis of faith and reason; one's own life must reflect this synthesis in daily tasks. The Virgin Mary, being a good neighbor, good mother, good educator, etc., lived being faithful in the little things in such a way that when she got to the much,That is to say, by accompanying her Son in the Passion, Death and Resurrection, she already had the practice of living from faith and reason and it was not strange for her to live those events with faith and reason. Her whole life reflected that synthesis. On the other hand, What-do-I-care, What-will-they-say, Rigorous and Fructuoso lived that synthesis - faith, reason, life - at certain moments. They left aside the mandate to be faithful in little things and put themselves in the hands of their own whim.

Mrs. Perfect

It's the limit! So much shouting at this time of night. I'm going to put order in this street! How much this street has changed since so many strangers have arrived! My God, give me patience! exclaimed Mrs. Perfecta. I'm close to retirement. I'll leave this disgusting and dangerous place as soon as I can, like all those that the police have just brought here. I hope they spend a good time in prison so they don't come back here. They deserve to be punished. I know these people. Oh! If only they knew what I know about them. I've watched them every night and noticed that they're involved in shady business. None of them are worth it. What will they say? He cheats on his partner, he only comes at night to see his girlfriend, more than that, his lover. What do I care? He sells illegal substances. He rides his bicycle who knows what at this time of night. Rigorous is a conceited, proud, arrogant man, he thinks he knows the law but he doesn't even know how to say hello in English. Fructuoso is a gossip, he has his YouTube channel and everything he sees is public. He makes a living from that. He's lazy, who would make a living from that! He doesn't even believe it. He lies to people.

Mrs. Perfect is a woman who suffers from insomnia. She entertains herself by observing the neighborhood during the nights when she can't sleep. She works in a supermarket, coordinates the dairy section and sometimes helps with the cash control at the end of the day. Her coworkers fear and detest her. She doesn't tolerate even a joke, you can't ask her age, much less where she lives even though everyone knows. She is of medium height, a little plump, of Italian descent, aquiline, divorced. She has four children but can't live with any of them. They barely greet her on her birthday. She boasts about her ancestors and despises those who don't have her skin color. She looks at them sideways and expresses her feelings with her gaze. She barely participates in social gatherings at work. She is stingy, ridiculous, and argues over the slightest difficulty. Her coworkers gave her the nickname Mrs. Perfect. She believes she has no flaws, that she doesn't make mistakes, and that she even finds justification for all the misdeeds she does. The other day they found her eating an apple in the fruit section, something that she herself forbids her coworkers to do, but she ends up making exceptions for herself. Her bosses have mixed feelings. On the one hand, they like her because she is precise in ordering dairy products, she is exact when closing the cash register, she doesn't tolerate any defect, but it also bothers them. Her unstable and toxic character questions them, but they don't fire her because they can't find a replacement that would allow them not to lose their income. On the weekends, Doña Perfecta helps at her Church. She is a volunteer. She has been volunteering for years. She finds a certain satisfaction and joy. However, she can't get along with the other employees. She barely speaks to a patient female volunteer named Sufrida. She immediately questions everything. The others murmur, saying, "She thinks she's perfect." No one confronts her because they think she is not worth it. They notice that discussions give her life and she can live in a hostile environment. To avoid all that, they let her believe that she is doing things well even though they know she is not. She has sometimes challenged the Pastor. She has put him in "check" at certain times. Supposedly, she believes that she knows everything. She knows how to educate children, she knows the laws, she knows the local language, what is good for young people or not. She knows what should be bought and what should not for the Church, etc. However, she remains in mere talk. She is a talkative and uncommitted. Religiously, she believes that she has the faith that no one else has. She lives the true religion. Faithful devotee of the Virgin Mary. She does not miss Mass. She believes she has taken on and lived in a very eloquent way what Luke says in his Gospel: "The seed that fell on good soil refers to those who, after hearing the Word with a noble and generous heart, retain it and bear fruit through their perseverance" (Lk 8:15). Perfecta believes that she embodies these words. She does not say it but she expresses it. Aware of her weaknesses, she tries to hide them, to silence them, and above all, she denies them. Sometimes she comes to her senses and reproaches herself, but it only lasts a few moments, then she goes back to her own thing. Why is it that Doña Perfecta is a "faithful believer" and her life continues to distort her faith? What is the true religion? Is religion perhaps a refuge for toxic people? Her friend Sufrida tries to understand her, invites her to her house, offers her food and good hospitality. She tells her that she suffers from low self-esteem, to which Perfecta responds by presenting her with the figure of the Virgin Mary. Obviously a distorted image of the Virgin. She tells her that the Virgin asks her to pray a lot, to get on her knees, to get up at 4 in the morning and do penance, however, she omits to mention an essential virtue of Mary: humility. It is not good for her to reflect on that virtue because she would have to change her life. If humility is not explained well, the Sufferer will sink even further and lose motivation to continue. People avoid talking about this virtue. Those who claim to be devoted to Mary without having a hint of humility at least have nothing to do with her. The Japanese philosopher Nishitani Keiji stated that "we can refer to the relationship between man and God as the abandonment of one's own will in order to live according to the will of God."[3]. Renouncing one's own will requires a high dose of humility. Furthermore, faith and reason must be in permanent dialogue in order to make one's own life a testimony of God's will. Whoever experiences the realization of God's will in his or her life could be said to have achieved the expected fruit that Saint Luke has spoken of. In the life of the Virgin Mary, one can observe the experience of God's will. Based on what God has said, she organizes her life. In her, humility, faith and reason are seen as virtues that guide her life. Doña Perfecta has closed herself off from exercising her reason and has stagnated in a faith that does not motivate her to change her life. It is difficult for a person who cannot control her life to practice calm reasoning and, therefore, mature in faith.

---

[3]N. Keiji, Religion and Nothingness, London, Oxford University Press, 1999, p. 42.

Lady Sufferer

Ring ring ring, the cell phone rings, it's Sufrida! says Mrs. Perfecta, she slides her iPhone 15 with her thumb, she is always up to date with technology, to answer the call. You hear moans, whimpers and small screams, what happened? What is happening? asks Perfecta. Sufrida with a trembling voice says, have you heard the news? They just started a war in the Middle East! Is that why you are calling me? says Perfecta. Don't you understand God's revelation? Don't you know that the Virgin has appeared and announced this disaster? continues Sufrida, don't you see that the end of the world is approaching? You are worried about mere nonsense! affirms Perfecta. You shouldn't be interested in this news so far away from us. Live your life! Don't worry about what doesn't affect you. Whether there is war or not, what about us? Can we intervene in this situation? Calm down! You better pray, take care of your husband and your children, live in peace. Don't call me for that! Suffering, she is worried and asks herself: is my friend right? Why did I call her? I am going to call her again to apologize. She calms down, goes to the garden of her house, begins to pray the Rosary and suddenly sees a wild cat that has caught a mouse. She begins to beg the cat to free the mouse, as if the cat could understand her. Without any success, the cat ends up killing the mouse. She begins to cry and honor her name, suffers and suffers, cries, exclaims: why is there so much evil in the world?! Surely it is the work of the devil. She immediately goes to the Church near her house. She makes the sign of the cross and in just a few minutes the Mass begins. In the homily the priest begins to rant against the evil in the world. Suffering tells herself, I am not wrong, however, it makes her doubt because the preacher begins to rant against devout women, criticizes appearances, talks to them about Disney, imagines Hollywood fashions and dreams of having a Church full of celebrities, well dressed, even himself dressed as a kind of prince full of people who follow him, serve him and flatter him. The reflection is spoiled and Suffering returns home worse than before. She reflects and says: I better read the gospel! Even the priests are contaminated! How awful!... She picks up her blue Bible, a little faded and dusty, cleans it and thinks, what does God want to tell me? I'm going to open the Bible at random, let's see what text comes out! That way I will know what God wants to tell me. She opens the Bible and that passage from Luke appears that says:

"In the sixth month the angel Gabriel was sent by God to a town in Galilee called Nazareth, to a virgin betrothed to a man whose name was Joseph… The virgin's name was Mary. When she came in, she said to her, 'Hail, full of favor, the Lord is with you! ' She was troubled by this and wondered what this greeting could mean. The angel said to her, 'Do not be afraid, Mary, for you have found favor with God. You will conceive in your womb and bear a son, and you shall name him Jesus… Mary said to the angel, 'How can this be, since I do not know a man? ' The angel answered her…" Lk 1:26-36.

When she read these words, Sufrida shuddered and thought that the angel was speaking to her. She questions herself, she worries and doesn't know what to do. Who could explain to me the text I just read? She said to herself. Her husband, Bartolo, arrives. He is a hard-working man, of medium height, a little overweight and not very religious. He asks her: What's wrong? She says: "I feel that God is speaking to me!" He remains silent and thinks in his mind: "This woman is crazy." I must do something! He calls his friend Clodomiro, Perfecta's husband, whom he considers to be a little educated and tells him everything that is happening to his wife. The friend tells him: women today are crazy! The same thing happens to my wife. She tells me about apparitions of the Virgin, about days of darkness that will soon occur and everything in an apocalyptic tone. I think that we should send them to a spiritual retreat or, at least, to a place where they can explain to them what is happening to them. Ah! The other day my son found an ad on the Internet that said: Marian Congress. Faith and Reason. Why don't we send them there? That way we'll be free for at least 4 days and we can rest, we can even agree and go out alone, without them and remember old times. Good idea! Now it's up to us to convince them that they should attend this congress. They agree and both, each in their own way, try to insist to their wives that religion is necessary and even more so to try to understand it. They promise that they want to learn from them as long as they attend this congress. The women communicate with each other and both say: Has God touched the hearts of our husbands? Are our prayers having an effect? They doubt but agree that their prayers are powerful and their husbands are "beginning" to live their faith. The husbands are happy that their wives have agreed to go to the congress. They both laugh, express their joy because "at least we'll be four days without them," what liberation and what happiness! Let's get organized and enjoy these! However, Sufrida senses that there is something that doesn't fit behind all this. These people are planning something! I'm not leaving! But she had already agreed with her friend that they would go and she couldn't break her word. Sufrida was a religious woman, she lived religion in her own way, with certain very special aspects. It was hard for her to think of a faith that would change her life or at least strengthen it. Finally, they get organized, buy the tickets to go to the congress, sign up and leave everything ready to travel. The day of the trip arrives, both with two suitcases as if they were going to be away from home for a year, they had their things well organized. In one suitcase everything that had to do with aesthetics: hair dryer, makeup, cleaning, etc., in the other suitcase clothes, even those they didn't need. Swimwear, and clothes to go out to party... the habit of always having everything left over. Accumulating material things without any sense and paying for excess weight in transportation simply because you don't know how to live with what is necessary.

Marian Congress, first conference: faith and reason in Mary

They arrive at the congress venue. Everything is very beautiful for them. Most of the participants were women, over 40 years old. They settle into their rooms, check the congress schedule and then prepare for the welcome session. More than 100 people had gathered from different parts of the world. Curiously, the initial presentation of the congress is given by a renowned philosopher-theologian and will precisely reflect on faith and reason in the Virgin Mary. Sufrida and her friend Perfecta are excited. They carry a notebook to take notes, they prepare their cell phone to record the session even though all the material will be given to all participants virtually.

The conference organizers introduce the speaker and he immediately begins his reflection. Coincidentally, he stops his presentation to reflect on the Annunciation of the angel to Mary according to Luke's account. All the participants are very attentive and murmured, saying, "This is very interesting. What is this reflection about?" He stops at the question of the Virgin Mary to the angel: How can this be since I do not know a man? Mary's question reflects the natural desire to know that the great philosopher Aristotle said, "Man by nature desires to know." It is a question of knowledge not only of natural things but also of supernatural reality. Mary's question reveals that an event like what happened to her goes beyond human reason and requires recourse to theology (faith). The Annunciation is beyond the reach of human intellect. Difficult to understand for human reason. A fact that should not be analyzed from reason alone but from faith. Faith seeks to understand and know so that God may guide thinking and acting. This attitude of Mary cannot be ignored when reflecting on faith and reason. Mary is a testimony of how it is possible to embody faith and reason in one life. In the 11th-12th century, Saint Anselm of Canterbury said "I believe in order to understand." In the case of the Virgin Mary, it would be "I believe in order to ask, I ask in order to believe." The humble attitude of the Virgin makes her have a broad vision that quickly embraces faith and, as a consequence, a new mystery occurs. Something about God is "understood" but then a new mystery arises to be investigated. Mary is aware of this because she answers: "Here is the handmaid of the Lord. What you say is fulfilled in me." Lk. 1:38. In Mary, a change takes place from the faith that questions to the faith that trusts. An encounter between faith and reason. The faith that questions made Mary serve God. What human reason does not understand must be kept "meditated in the heart" (2:19). Mary kept in her heart all the words of the angel, of the shepherds, of the wise men, and of all the manifestations of God. She meditated on those words and they served to shape her entire lifestyle and her way of being. Perhaps, at the moment she heard them she did not fully understand them, but she meditated on the words and from them she put into practice everything that God was indicating to her. Mary's life was shaped or oriented by faith and reason, or from a simple faith to a thoughtful faith. Faith is lived in meditation based on reason and faith. The underlying issue that Mary's life reveals to us is, ultimately, the relationship between God and man; the search for union between faith and reason is the task of every believer. Mary's faith reflects confidence in the midst of uncertainties and doubts, in the midst of threats, blackmail and sometimes bribery from those around her.Reasoned faith frees life from fear or at least controls it. This reflection ends by inviting participants to share and discuss in a group the importance of the Virgin in the life of every believer.

After the presentation, Sufrida and her friend are happy but have many questions: How should I live, only with faith or only with reason? How can I integrate faith and reason in my life? They talk to each other and share their notes, stating: The Virgin Mary embodies an exemplary synthesis between full trust in the divine and the capacity for human reflection in the face of the mysteries that life presents. Mary is a model of faith because she freely accepts the divine plan at the moment of the Annunciation (Lk 1:38). Her response to the angel, "Let it be done to me according to your word," shows an active and conscious disposition. It is not an act of blind obedience, but of trust in the mystery of God, which is gradually revealed to her. Thomas Aquinas affirms that reason is a divine light in man, and Mary shows how this light can be perfectly integrated with faith. By accepting her role as Mother of God, Mary freely assumes her place in the plan of salvation, demonstrating that faith does not cancel reason, but rather fulfills it. She does not seek to impose her will on the divine plan, but neither does she abdicate her freedom. As Edith Stein points out, Mary is a model of a person in whom reason and faith are not in conflict, but work together to live a fully human life open to the divine.[4]. His example shows that true wisdom does not lie in choosing between faith or

---

[4]Cf. A. MacIntyre, Edith Stein. A Philosophical Prologue (1913-1922), Granda, Nuevo Inicio, 2008.

reason, but in allowing both to work together to reach the truth and the ultimate meaning of life. His figure dialogues perfectly with philosophical concerns, inviting us to rethink the relationship between the divine and the human.[5]. Suffering and Perfecta are going to take advantage of the break time to enter the next conference, in the meantime, they dedicate themselves to dialogue.

---

[5]Cf. I. Gómez-Acebo (ed.), And you, who do you say that I am?, In a woman's key, Bilbao, Desclée de Brouwer, 2000.

Cáemebien and Doblada

During this break, they meet two women who were walking alone, each on their own, but they join Sufrida and her friend. One was called Caémebien and the other Doblada. Caémebien, around 50 years old, is a woman who walks through life with her head held high and her ego swollen like a balloon on the verge of bursting. She proclaims herself "more beautiful than roses" and is convinced that others envy her for her supposed perfection, although reality paints a very different picture. Her teeth, yellowed and crooked, tell stories of neglect and years of candy devoured with carelessness, and her gaze, always evasive and suspicious, arouses more distrust than admiration. Despite her lack of popularity - or perhaps because of it - Caémebien has an excessive obsession with being the center of attention and dreams of ruling everyone as if she were an uncrowned queen. But her personality, sharp as a malicious knife, makes her a figure detested by those who have the misfortune of crossing her path. She is always up to something, using emotional blackmail as her weapon of choice, and her attempts at manipulation are as obvious as a disguise in broad daylight. The curious thing is that Caémebien does not realize how others perceive her. She continues to believe that with the simple power of her presence she can conquer hearts and minds, although all she achieves is a chorus of eyes rolling towards the sky. However, beneath that facade of arrogance, there is an abyss of insecurities that she tries to fill with fantasies of greatness and contempt for anyone who does not recognize her "majesty." Her tragedy, and her comedy, lies in the fact that the world continues to turn without noticing her existence, while she is desperate to be someone she can never be. She is "religious", she loves flowers and makes arrangements in the Church, however, her life is divided, her faith and her reason. Instead, Doblada is a woman around 55 years old, living in a permanent emotional twilight, trapped between nostalgia for what could have been and the fear of facing what really is. Her melancholy has no poetic nuances; it is rather a gray and damp weight that envelops her and conditions each of her decisions. She has a catastrophic mentality, always expecting the worst to happen, which leads her to sabotage any possibility of happiness before it even appears on her horizon. Her mood depends exclusively on the attention she receives. She is an expert in the art of drama, capable of turning a simple slight into a personal apocalypse. Doblada is a puppet in the hands of time; she lets it pass without direction or purpose, always waiting for something or someone to come and rescue her from herself. However, that wait is not passive: it is active in its chaos. Since she was young, she has sought to fill her inner emptiness with an endless parade of lovers,adventures that began as escapes and ended as labyrinths. Her marriage, a pact of convenience rather than love, was doomed from the start, and her infidelities soon became part of her routine. With her latest lover, the tragedy reached a new depth. Discovering that not even furtive passion could cure her dissatisfaction, Doblada made him her scapegoat, the recipient of all her guilt and resentment. In her reproaches she accuses him of having destroyed her life, when in reality, her unhappiness is a work that she herself has built brick by brick. Religious in ritual but atheist in spirituality, Doblada attends Mass and prays fervently, but she does so more as a staging to reaffirm her role in the drama than as a true act of faith. For her, God is a judge who must be appeased, but in whom she neither trusts nor hopes. Her relationship with religion is a reflection of her life: full of contradictions, marked by appearances and empty of meaning. Doblada is a tragic character disguised as a comedy. Her name, almost caricature-like, evokes both the sadness of her twisted life and the irony of her existence: always seeking to straighten out a destiny that she herself is determined to twist.

These two characters join the group of Sufrida and her friend. They already know each other's stories, they all complain and it seems that they all suffer, but none of them like Sufrida. They try to talk about the conference they just heard, but neither of them wants to go into detail because deep down they know that the only ones responsible for their current situation are themselves. They don't want to go into themselves, they want to look for those responsible for their moods and their own decisions. They don't accept that each one is the result of their decisions, their decisions reflect their situation. It becomes an endless discussion and dialogue between them, but they must go to the other conference. However, they begin to feel that there are more people in the world who experience the same thing.

Clodomiro and Bartolo, finally free?

Bartolo and Clodomiro, two men whom fate had brought together through the friendship of their wives, found themselves in an unusual situation: their respective wives, Sufrida and Perfecta, were out of town, attending spiritual conferences (Marian congress). It was as if the air in their homes had changed density; for the first time in a long time, they breathed a different oxygen, less laden with expectations and judgments. Bartolo, Sufrida's husband, was a man of light spirit, happy by nature, although aware that his marriage was a constant emotional challenge. Sufrida, as her name suggested, had a tragic soul, prone to magnifying problems and sailing in an ocean of laments. However, Bartolo accepted her as she was, with a mixture of loving resignation and a humor that served as his lifeline. For him, those days of "temporary bachelorhood" were a necessary respite, a reminder that he could also enjoy his own space. Clodomiro, on the other hand, was the husband of Perfecta, a woman whose name seemed to be a cruel joke of fate. Perfecta was not so much perfect as she was controlling, a master in the art of gently dominating Clodomiro, who had adopted a docile role in their relationship to avoid conflict. While Clodomiro was not unhappy, he lived in a constant search for solutions to keep the peace, sacrificing in the process his own desires and autonomy. During this marital break, the two friends decided to take advantage of the time to disconnect from their routines. They went to Mass together, an act they normally performed under the watchful eye of their wives, but which this time they did of their own free will. To their surprise, listening to the homily without feeling the pressure of an imposed duty was refreshing, even liberating. Later, they prepared a simple meal and set out for a nearby lake to fish, enjoying an afternoon that seemed straight out of a movie about male camaraderie. Upon returning, with the twilight tinting the sky orange and their hearts light from the day they had shared, Bartolo and Clodomiro sat down to have a few drinks. It was then that the conversation, fueled by the effect of alcohol and the trust between them, took an unexpected turn. Both confessed something they had hidden even from themselves: they had been unfaithful. Bartolo expressed it with a certain light guilt, almost like someone admitting to having broken a promise from their youth. Clodomiro, on the other hand, said it with a tone of deep shame, as if he had just released a weight he had been carrying for years. They tried to justify their actions, using arguments that seemed unconvincing even to themselves. But, finally, they admitted that they had failed. The conversation turned to their marriages. Both agreed that their wives, each in their own way, had invaded their lives of faith,trying to impose on them ways of believing and living the faith that were not natural to them. "It's not that I don't believe in God," Bartolo said, "but sometimes I feel that she believes more in ritual than in love." Clodomiro nodded, adding: "I go to Mass for her, but I don't know if that counts. I prefer not to insist on the subject so as not to fight, but I feel that something of me is lost in that silence." At the end of the night, the two men said goodbye with a handshake and an ambiguous sentiment. They had discovered that they shared more than they thought: the burden of asymmetrical relationships, the weight of wrong decisions and the struggle to keep the peace in marriages that, although functional, were far from ideal. However, they also shared something more valuable: the ability to reflect, to confess and, perhaps, to begin to seek a balance that would allow them to be faithful, not only to their wives, but also to themselves.

Second conference:
Mary in the plan of salvation

The lecturer opens his lecture with this quotation: "After experience had taught me that all the things which frequently occur in ordinary life are vain and futile, and seeing that all these things were for me the cause and object of fear, and contained in themselves neither good nor evil, except in so far as my mind was affected by them, I finally resolved to inquire whether there was anything which was a true and communicable good, and of such a nature that, by itself, all other things being rejected, it would affect the mind; nay, whether there was anything which, if found and possessed, would give me eternal joy and continual supreme joy. I say I finally resolved, because at first sight it seemed imprudent to want to give up one certain thing for another which was still uncertain. For I saw the advantages which come from honour and riches, and that I was forced to give them up if I wished to devote myself seriously to a new task. Hence, if supreme happiness lay in them, I necessarily lacked it; And if, on the contrary, I did not reside in them and I devoted myself exclusively to their search, I would equally lack supreme happiness."[6].

What do we need to save ourselves from? From seeking passing goods and dedicating ourselves to seeking a true good that provides continuous and supreme joy? In this plan of salvation, Mary was an essential element. Let us look more closely.

The Bible tells us an essential and profound truth: all of humanity needs to be saved. This message, which runs through the Scriptures, is not always obvious to people, and a key question arises: what do we need to be saved from? The answer refers us to a concept that is presented as the axis of our human condition: sin and its consequences. Understanding this is not only an act of faith, but a reflective and existential process that leads us to look at our lives honestly. Sin is not just an abstraction or a theological concept; it is something that we experience in a palpable way in our lives. Who among us has not felt the wound of injustice? Let us think about the impact of a theft, a lie, or a betrayal. When someone deceives us with empty promises, something inside us tells us

---

[6]B. Spinoza, Treatise on the Reform of the Understanding. Descartes' Principles of Philosophy. Metaphysical Thoughts, Madrid, Alianza, 2022, pp. 97-98.

that "this is not right." In these moments, we not only identify the fault of the other, but also the harm that this fault causes us. Even the most crime-hardened seek to surround themselves with people who will tell them the truth, because at the very core of the human condition, no one can bear to live under the weight of lies. Yet sin is not only manifested when we are victims, but also when we are the guilty ones. We face the remorse that comes from looking at the consequences of our own actions. A parent who sees their children caught up in addictions or destructive behaviors may think, "I failed as a parent, I didn't know how to lead my family." This kind of guilt reflects how sin transcends the individual and affects our relationships, leaving a trail of pain, confusion, and loss. In these human experiences of injustice and remorse, we find the first clues to what sin really means: a burden that oppresses, a shadow that separates us from the light, a poison that steals joy and hope. The story of salvation—God's design to free us from this situation—is seen throughout his Word. From the earliest accounts of the Bible, God shows us that we are not left at the mercy of this darkness. The history of salvation reveals to us a divine plan that unfolds in three fundamental steps:

First, enlighten our conscience: God, through Moses and the prophets, shows us what is good and what is bad. The Ten Commandments, for example, are not mere rules, but a guide to living in harmony with God and with others. They are like signs along the way, marking the limits so that we do not stray into chaos and, above all, to avoid returning to slavery.

Second. Discovering our powerlessness: The law alone is not enough. It is in our inability to fully comply with it that we discover our weakness. This discovery is not a condemnation, but an opportunity to recognize our need for help. Peter, in asking Jesus how many times he should forgive, shows this internal struggle: "Lord, I am willing, but there is a limit I cannot overcome."

Third: Receiving redemption through Jesus Christ: Here God's work culminates. By sending us his Son, he offers us not only forgiveness, but also the strength to overcome that which enslaves us. Jesus is not only the Lamb who takes away the sin of the world, but also the one who transforms our heart of stone into a heart of flesh, full of life and love.

Now, if we carefully analyze the Holy Scriptures, particularly the historical books, we will see that the people fell into three temptations: to secure prosperity, to generate pleasure and to practice greed. The Old Testament describes the people of Israel facing three great temptations that, far from being ancient, resonate in our contemporary reality:

Ensuring prosperity: The Israelites built altars to the Baals, gods of fertility and the earth, seeking to ensure abundant harvests. At its core, this revealed a lack of trust in God. Today, this temptation manifests itself in an obsession with economic security and materialism. The Israelites said to themselves: God has not freed them from slavery in Egypt, but He does not know how to cultivate the land or care for livestock, so let us turn to those gods.

Pleasure: The excessive enjoyment of life led to disorders and excesses among God's people. In our society, this translates into addictions to consumption, entertainment, and an insatiable search for personal satisfaction. The neighbor who suffers or is in a vulnerable situation does not count; only tranquility, feeling good, and doing what pleases each one of us matters. Many times doing what we like means doing what we don't like. If you own a company, you may like it, but it is unpleasant to have to tell an employee that he can work harder or that he is fired. Those who dedicate themselves to pleasure do not understand or are not aware of what it means to dedicate themselves only to doing what they like.

Greed: The desire to accumulate more and more led to injustice and exploitation of the poor. The corruption that permeates so many social and political structures today is nothing more than a continuation of this dynamic. Greed manifests itself in many ways, from small everyday actions to major crimes that affect an entire society. A contemporary example might be that of a businessman who, despite possessing an immense fortune, exploits his workers to increase his profits. Imagine this businessman, owner of a large chain of factories, who decides to reduce wages and increase the working hours of his employees, even though he already has enough resources to live comfortably for himself and his descendants for generations. In addition, he invests in marketing campaigns to present a charitable image to the public, while secretly evading taxes through tax havens. This businessman does not need more money to live, but his insatiable desire to accumulate wealth leads him to commit injustices that impoverish others. His greed not only separates him from his employees, whom he should care for as part of a community, but it also isolates him from God, as he prioritizes material accumulation over spiritual and human values. In this example we see how greed not only affects the greedy, but destroys the social fabric, generates inequality and dehumanizes relationships.

It is a spiritual trap that steals inner peace and connection with others, leaving the person trapped in an existential void that no material good can fill.

These temptations are ultimately distractions that draw us away from God and plunge us into a cycle of perpetual dissatisfaction. Faced with our failures, we often fall into a false solution: the religion of compromise. It is the idea that we can "negotiate" with God, appeasing him with external acts while our hearts remain unchanged. Jeremiah denounced this attitude: "Your sacrifices are detestable because your life does not change." This religion anesthetizes our conscience, but it does not transform our lives. Today, this anesthesia takes many forms: The normalization of sin: "Everyone does it, why not me?"; superficial practices: meditation that soothes, but does not transform. The cult of individual rights: "I have the right to enjoy my life," we say, while ignoring the consequences of those decisions. Yet God always awakens us. He awakened his people through banishment, something excessively tragic, yet it served to change the hearts of the people. The exile to Babylon led them to see the truth of sin[7].

---

[7]Jeremiah 26:1-9. For those who want to go deeper, it would be good to analyze the historical books: Joshua,

The Bible shows us that when God's people fell into these traps, exile came. It was a painful awakening, a complete stripping away of anesthesia and false security. In exile, there was no prosperity, pleasure or accumulation possible; only the naked truth of their dependence on God remained. In our lives, this "exile" can manifest itself as moments of crisis: loss, failure, or confrontation with our own fragility. It is there that we hit rock bottom and discover our need for God. This painful process is also a grace, because it allows us to be reborn as the "poor of Yahweh," those who do not trust in the powers of this world, but only in God. They did not expect anything from human beings other than from God. It is up to us to live out that attitude. As St. Paul teaches: "When I am weak, then I am strong, because the power of Christ dwells in me." The recognition of our weakness is not a reason for despair, but the first step toward true strength, which only comes from God. The biblical message is to learn to recognize our weakness and to know who has the power. The weaker I am, the greater the power of God shines in me. This happened to those who no longer depended on any human power, but on God. Salvation, then, is not just a theological concept, but a living reality that

---

Judges, Ruth, Samuel (1 and 2); Kings (1 and 2); Chronicles, Ezra, Nehemiah, Tobit, Judith, Esther.

transforms our being. It is the process by which God returns us to the fullness for which we were created, freeing us from sin and opening us to a life in communion with Him. In this history of salvation, each one of us has a unique role, and the response we give to this call will be the echo of our eternity. Thus the conference ends. The speaker invites group and personal dialogue. The women together again are going to discuss the conference, which had touched them because now they had to dedicate themselves to seeking the Good that never ends.

When words echo

The sky above the conference venue was grey, a silent omen that reflected the interior of Sufrida, Perfecta, Doblada and Cáemebien. They had come to the spiritual retreat with different intentions, although none of them would admit it openly. Faith, for them, was more of a habit than a transformation as seen in each one's personality. They prayed the Rosary, yes, but the days slipped by between routines and empty prayers, as if God were a spectator in their lives, and not the protagonist. They decided to talk about the conference and Perfecta took the floor and said: I'm going to read my notes just in case you forgot the conference so we'll have everything fresher to talk about, Perfecta begins by reading her notes, they wanted to stray from the subject and Perfecta believes what her name supposedly is and forces them to listen to her and begins:

The speaker, with a firm and compassionate voice, spoke about the people of Israel before their exile. They were a people full of greed, dedicated to pleasure and prosperity at all costs. But exile had stripped them of everything and, in that material and spiritual nakedness, they had found God again. From that purified people, Mary, the Virgin, emerged, an example of faith that did not stop at empty words, but transformed lives. "Mary's people had to lose everything to open their eyes. What will God have to take from us for us to really let him in?" The words fell like stones on the souls of the four women. End of Perfecta's summary.

*Suffered*She sighed, uncomfortable in her chair. She had come to the retreat seeking peace for her heart. She was saddled with a marriage full of recriminations and a life that made her feel like a shadow. She thought of her husband, a man absent more by choice than by circumstance. "He needs to hear this," she told herself to soothe the sting in her conscience. But as the days went by, an uncomfortable thought grew in her: What if I'm the one who needs to change?

Perfect. Always upright and composed, she looked down on the others with a certain condescension. Everything in her life was under control: the house was tidy, the prayers said at the right moment, and her role as mother and wife played out like a textbook. But the idea that Mary came from a village full of flaws disturbed her. "What does that have to do with us?" she murmured after the lecture. Yet the speaker's words kept hammering home: "True faith does not perfect the appearance, it transforms the heart."

Folded. She lived with a resignation disguised as faith. Her marriage was a game of silences, her life a joyless heap of duties. Hearing about the exiled people reminded her of her own sense of loss. She had stopped expecting anything from life, from her husband, even from God. In a moment of sincerity during the conversation, she murmured: "Sometimes I think I pray because it is easier than changing."

Fall in love with me, always "smiling" and "friendly," was the one who sparked the conversation in the pauses. But behind her laughter was a marriage broken by appearances. Her husband was more interested in success than in her, and Cáemebien had learned to hide her pain behind jokes. Proud of herself more out of conviction than out of pity and sorrow for herself. The conference made her deeply uncomfortable. "How can I admit that our life needs so much change?" she thought. But that night, praying the rosary, she felt that the words were more a cry for help than a habit.

The four women were left wondering that to some extent they regretted having come to the conferences. They did not want to accept the Virgin Mary, they were faithful devotees, but they did not know her. They did not think that being a devotee of the Virgin implies a constant conversion, a change of life. After experiencing these feelings, the four women met together again after the conference. At first, they talked about trivial things. But soon, the speaker's words emerged.

"I don't like what you say," Sufrida confessed, breaking the ice. "I'd rather just pray. This whole changing thing... it's too much."

"Yes," Perfecta agreed. "I do enough for my family, what more is expected of me?"

—But... what if he's right? —Doblada intervened, with a timidity that surprised the others—. What if our faith hasn't changed us because we don't want to change?

*Fall in love with me*He remained silent. He looked at the three of them and finally confessed:

—Praying is easy. But changing... changing is another thing. I have never wanted to look inside myself. Maybe that's why my husband and I are the way we are.

The four of them remained silent, feeling that something was moving within them. Before continuing with the next conference, there was a space for adoration of the Blessed Sacrament. During the adoration, the speaker's words became real in their hearts: "Mary was not the same after saying 'yes' to God. Faith transforms or it is not faith." Sufrida stopped thinking about how much her husband needed to change and began to think about how much she needed to change. Perfecta realized that her perfection was a shield, not a fruit of love. Doblada understood that her resignation was not faith, but fear. Cáemebien felt that she could face her wounds instead of hiding them behind a smile and pride that prevented her from speaking to others. They were beginning to understand that the Virgin Mary was a mother who came from a town purified by pain, and now she seemed closer to them, more human, more real. When they left the adoration, the four of them knew that the journey had just begun. They prayed the Rosary, yes, but now with a new intention: to transform their lives and that of their families from within. Because, as they told them at the conferences, faith that does not change life is just an empty ritual. It was time to go to the next conference and Doblada began to feel panic attacks, she remembered her stormy past and began to shout: no more secrets! from now on I am going to free myself from secrets, however, they were just shouts of someone carried away by emotion, it was time to show it in everyday life. The same happened with the others, Perfecta no longer wanted to go to the conference because she said that it was enough for her, no more questioning, however, Sufrida encouraged the others and told them let's take advantage of being here and really get to know who the Virgin Mary is. The others nodded.

Third conference: spirituality of the Anawin (poor of Yahweh)

The conference began with a disconcerting question that resonated in the hearts of those in attendance: "Poverty according to the Bible or according to me?" The silence in the room was almost tangible. It was a simple question in its formulation, but devastating in its implication. The speaker went on, in a firm but compassionate voice, to explain that the answer to this question was not just an intellectual exercise, but a revelation about the lifestyle each person was willing to adopt. Poverty, according to Scripture, was not simply material lack, but a radical attitude of total trust in God. "Poor," he continued, "is he who does not trust in the powers of this world, but relies fully on the promises of God. He is he who expects nothing from men, but everything from God. He is he whose heart is connected to the Creator, even in the midst of suffering and humiliation."

With this introduction, the speaker directed the audience's attention to the figure of Mary, the Virgin of Nazareth, who reflected the spirituality of the Anawin, the poor of Yahweh. He explained that the

Anawin were those who, from the depths of their misery, had not succumbed to discouragement, but had placed their hope in God. Mary, a humble young woman from an insignificant village, embodied this spirituality. "Can anything good come out of Nazareth?" she asked rhetorically, quoting the words of Nathanael. Nazareth, located in Galilee, was a despised region, a land considered lost and mixed with the Gentiles. However, it was precisely from there that God chose the mother of His Son. "Mary is the poor woman of Nazareth," he explained, "she who did not trust in herself, but lived in absolute dependence on the will of God." The speaker cited three biblical texts to illustrate this spirituality: the song of Hannah in 1 Samuel 2, Psalm 111, and Mary's Magnificat. Each of these, he said, reflects how the humble are exalted by God while the proud are humbled. "Mary," he said, "is the perfect model of the Beatitudes; she is the new 'nothing' from which God does His work." God created from nothing and He creates us anew from our 'nothing' as He did with Mary.

The discussion then turned to the marriage between Mary and Joseph. The speaker explained that in Jewish tradition, marriage was a marital commitment as binding as marriage itself. Although the couple did not yet live together, they were already considered husband and wife, and infidelity at this stage was considered adultery. "Each man's word was his commitment," he stressed, contrasting this reality with modern relationships where, many times, intimacy precedes formal commitment. In this context, the speaker addressed Mary's question at the angel's announcement: "How will this be, since I do not know man?" Since St. John Chrysostom, he explained, this question has been interpreted as a reference to the purpose of virginity that Mary had adopted with Joseph. If Mary had not had this purpose, her question would not make sense, since a married woman would naturally expect to have children. But Mary, upon receiving the announcement, faced a monumental dilemma: accepting God's will meant risking her honor, her reputation and possibly her life. "Mary trusted completely in God," the speaker said, "even when the path was uncertain and dangerous."

The speaker delved deeper into the mystery of the Incarnation, explaining that Christ was formed solely from Mary's body, but that Joseph, as Mary's husband, participated spiritually in this mystery. "We cannot reduce Joseph to an adoptive or putative father," he clarified. "Joseph and Mary were one flesh by their marriage. Mary's body, from which Christ was formed, also belonged to Joseph by virtue of their sacramental union." He stressed that the Holy Spirit did not come to displace Joseph, but to sanctify the love between him and Mary. "Jesus," he said emphatically, "is a gift to both. Mary is a virginal mother and Joseph is a virginal father. Their union was consecrated and blessed by God."

The conference concluded with a theological reflection on Mary's role as the new "nothing." The speaker compared the creation of the world to the Incarnation of Christ. In creation, God made everything from nothing. In the Incarnation, he explained, God made the new creation out of Mary's absolute humility and availability. "Mary is absolute transparency," he said. "In her there is no barrier that stops the light of God. She is the summary of all the defeats of the devil and all the triumphs of God."[8]."

---

[8]"We can refer to man's relationship with God as the abandonment of one's own will to live according to God's will, or as the vision or knowledge of God, or as the revelation of God in oneself." N. Keiji, Religion and Nothingness, Madrid, Siruela, 1999, p. 49. Mary is a testimony of renunciation of one's own will to be guided by God's will, the same occurs with the theme of nothingness (nihility). We are "nothing," at the end of our life we are reduced to nothing, however, God creates from nothing. Our conversion begins when we empty ourselves of ourselves, of all resentment, rancor, selfishness, etc… and being empty so that God occupies that place, therefore, it happens that the problem of "nothing" is solved from

The speaker closed with an invitation to follow Mary's example. "Our conversion begins when we empty ourselves," he said. "When we leave behind our resentment, pride and selfishness, we allow God to occupy that space. Mary teaches us that true greatness is found in humility and total trust in God."

The lecture left the audience in deep silence, not for lack of interest, but because every word seemed to strike a chord in their souls. The women began to murmur among themselves, uncomfortable with what they had heard. It was not easy to accept a message that challenged them to change not only their habits, but also their hearts. Yet, in the midst of the discomfort, some began to wonder if this was not the path to a more authentic faith. "Maybe," said one of them, "what we need is not to pray more, but to pray better. To change, like Mary, and to empty ourselves so that God can fill us."

"nothing." This model represents in some way the Virgin Mary.

Women's voices and Mary as a path

The room was filled with a peculiar air, a mixture of reflection and expectation. After listening to the lecture, the women began to talk among themselves, no longer with the voices filled with haste or judgment that they had brought when they arrived, but with calmer, almost introspective tones. There was something in Maria's message about "nothingness" that had touched them deeply, although in different ways. Sufrida was the first to break the silence, as always. Her name was not literal, but it was a kind of seal with which she identified herself. "Nothingness..." she began, as if testing the weight of those words in her mouth. "It's strange, isn't it? I've always felt that my life is a collection of things that weigh me down: pain, disappointment, worries. I had never thought of emptying myself of all that. I hold on to my sufferings so tightly that I leave no room for anything else... How do you let go?" Her eyes searched for answers in the air, but she found them in the others. Perfect, always impeccable, always in control, she sighed deeply. It was rare for her to speak without measuring her words, but this time she did. "Maybe starting by not trying to be so many things at the same time. I have always believed that if I am not the perfect mother, the perfect worker, the perfect daughter… I am failing. But now I think that maybe all that is just noise. Maria was not looking to be perfect, she was only looking to be transparent, available. Maybe that is what it means to trust in God. Not in my own strength, but in what He wants to do with me." The others looked at her, surprised by her frankness, but nodded silently. Bent over, as they affectionately called her, because she always seemed to shrink to give space to others, she looked up shyly. "It is so hard for me to think about that nothingness. Because to be honest, sometimes I feel like I am nothing. I live doing everything for others and I almost never think about myself. But what the speaker said… that God creates from nothingness… that gave me hope." Maybe being nothing doesn't mean disappearing, but rather being an open space for God to do something new." Cáemebien, who always seemed to have a smile ready for everyone, intervened with her usual energy, but this time more serene. "I think the most beautiful thing about all this is that no matter how we are or how much we have done, there is always an opportunity to start over. I loved that about emptying ourselves of resentment, of selfishness, of everything that hurts us. Imagine how free we could be if we did that. We would be like

Maria! Well, or at least we would try." There was a soft laugh in the group, a moment of relaxation. The message, which at first had seemed so dense, now slipped into their minds and hearts with a clarity that surprised them. "Don't you think this talk would have done Que dicenn y Que me importa a lot of good?" asked Sufrida, drawing more frank laughter. "Yes," answered Perfecta. "They are always caught up in what others think.It would have been helpful for them to hear that in the end we are nothing and that that is okay. That when we leave everything that weighs us down and open ourselves to God, we find what really matters." The conversation drifted off, but each one, in silence, began to think about her own life and how to apply what she had learned. Sufrida wondered how to let go of the pain she had been carrying for so long. Perfecta considered the possibility of letting go of her obsession with control. Dobladita dreamed of stopping hiding behind others and trusting that God was calling her to something more. Cáemebien felt the desire to share this message with other people, with that joy that always characterized her. The echo of the speaker's words remained in the air. In the end, they all agreed on one thing: Maria was not simply an unattainable model; she was an invitation to live in another way. A way that, although it challenged their certainties and fears, also promised something that none of them could ignore: the freedom to fully trust in God. The lectures began to change the way they looked at themselves and at others, but in their hearts the question echoed: and now that we are back home, what will become of us? Our husbands will not recognize us. If the first lecture touched them deeply and they did not want to change, in this second lecture they began to keep silent and seriously think about whether they are really devoted to the Virgin Mary. Without further comment they dispersed and at the time of the next lecture they arrived without discussion and occupied the first places. Their interest in Mary was increasing.If the first lecture touched them deeply and they did not want to change, then at this second lecture they began to keep silent and seriously think about whether they were really devoted to the Virgin Mary. Without further comment they dispersed and at the time of the next lecture they arrived without discussion and took the first places. Their interest in Mary was increasing.If the first lecture touched them deeply and they did not want to change, then at this second lecture they began to keep silent and seriously think about whether they were really devoted to the Virgin Mary. Without further comment they dispersed and at the time of the next lecture they arrived without discussion and took the first places. Their interest in Mary was increasing.

Fourth conference: Mary, servant of God and of her people

The fourth conference begins in a direct and clear manner: In the Scriptures we find four moments in which Mary is presented to us as a servant par excellence: the Visitation, the Wedding at Cana, her presence at the cross and at Pentecost. These passages not only reflect her life, but are an invitation to live service with depth and meaning.

The Visitation: Service that springs from love. Mary does not wait to be told what to do. Her heart, full of love and grace, acts with an initiative that is the reflection of a helpful soul. The angel does not order her to visit Elizabeth. There is no heavenly command that tells her: "Go, help your cousin who needs it." Nevertheless, Mary sets out. Not because she is asked to, but because the love that dwells in her does not allow indifference. True service is born from the abundance of a loving heart. Those who love do not wait to be asked for help, nor do they find excuses not to act. Mary carries with her something much greater than her presence: she carries God himself. And this is a key lesson. People do not need us; they need us to be bearers of God. If we forget this, we could rob God of His rightful place. Mary does not present herself as a protagonist, but as a servant. In our lives, service must be guided by a simple question: What is needed here? It is not a question of protagonism or control, but of being instruments. If we are parents, we have been given the mission of forming saints for God. If we are friends, we are called to be support and witness. In every relationship and circumstance, we are invited to reflect the divine love that dwells within us.

The Wedding at Cana: The measure of service is happiness. At Cana, Mary is no stranger to the needs of others. With a unique sensitivity, she perceives the lack of wine and takes the initiative to intercede. It is important to note that wine was not a matter of life or death. If there had been no wine, the spouses would still be married. However, Mary teaches us that service is not limited to what is strictly necessary; service seeks the fullness of happiness. Jesus performs his first miracle not to resolve an emergency, but to show that the happiness of others is also important to God. This teaches us that service goes beyond solving problems; its true objective is to bring joy, comfort and hope. Parents, for example, are not content with meeting the basic needs of their children. They want to see them happy. Happiness, in this sense, becomes a shield against sin, a fortress that protects the soul. A happy husband or wife hardly falls into temptations that destroy their relationship. Learning to serve to the point of achieving happiness for others is a way of reflecting God's love. However, service also involves letting go. Mary, even when interceding at Cana, does not control the results. She leaves everything in Jesus' hands. Serving is not imposing or suffocating with expectations; it is respecting the freedom of others and trusting that God will do what is best.

At the foot of the Cross: A service of permanence and reconciliation. Mary at the foot of the cross is an example of service at its best. She is not there out of obligation or for prominence, but because she loves. In that place of pain, she becomes a witness to union, reconciliation and sacrifice. Mary does not deny God, nor does she complain about his will, even though everyone around her abandons or betrays him. Her service at this moment is not active, but of presence and fidelity. She remains, silently supporting the suffering of the Son and of humanity.

At Pentecost, when the disciples gather together, she does not rebuke them for abandoning Jesus. There is no trace of vengeance in her heart, only acceptance and a faith that sustains others. Mary demonstrates with her life that the Gospel is possible. Even in the deepest pain, service can be an offering of love, a way of bearing witness that God is present and acting in our lives.

Mary as a model of the Holy Spirit working in her. Mary's life shows us how to recognize the work of the Holy Spirit in a person. Her life is marked by five characteristics that are clear signs of his action:

The fruits of her life: "By their fruits you will know them." Mary's greatest fruit is Jesus, the incarnation of divine love. She is blessed among all women because she allowed the Holy Spirit to work in her in a unique way.

Living the Gospel: Mary not only heard the Gospel; she lived it. Her "yes" to the angel and her fidelity in the beatitudes are proof that the Holy Spirit transformed her life into an offering.

Gratitude and mercy: Gratitude is another sign of the Holy Spirit. Mary does not seek rewards or follow the logic of transactions. Her life is marked by selfless giving, a reflection of God's unconditional love.

A constant life of virtue: Mary embodies the cardinal and theological virtues, with humility as their foundation. She is the perfect model of justice, prudence, fortitude, temperance, faith, hope and charity.

Bearing fruit in others: Mary's life transforms those who come close to her. Just as the little shepherds of Fatima found strength and comfort in her in the face of persecution, we too are called to be witnesses who inspire and transform lives.

Service gives meaning to life. Mary teaches us that serving is not just a task; it is a way of living. By emptying ourselves, renouncing our selfishness and resentment, and giving ourselves to others, we find true joy. Imitating Mary is not an unattainable ideal; it is an invitation to live with a heart open to the Holy Spirit, always seeking the one thing necessary: to love and serve God through our brothers and sisters. Mary, in her simplicity and greatness, reminds us that the true measure of service is love, and that in that love we find the purpose of our existence.

The martyrdom of Bartolo and Clodomiro

It was a warm, bright afternoon in the small town of San Gregorio del Arroyo. In the main square, two figures, who had gone for a stroll, sat under the shade of a leafy mango tree, accompanied by a freshly brewed coffee and an anxiety that seemed heavier than the humid air that surrounded them. Bartolo and Clodomiro, lifelong friends, shared a problem that united them more than any other in their lives: their wives were about to return from the Marian congress.

—I'm telling you, Bartolo, I've been at peace since they left —confessed Clodomiro, running his hand through his disheveled hair—. The house is quieter, I've eaten when I want, I've had my drinks without anyone looking at me with a judgmental look. I even finished that piece of furniture that I've been wanting to do for months!

*Bartolo*He nodded gravely, with his arms crossed and the expression of someone who carries the pains of a martyr on his shoulders.

—Me too, buddy. Ever since Sufrida came out with her Bible and her suitcase, I've slept like a king.

The TV on full blast, my socks where I want them… and not a single question about why I left my plate on the table! They both sighed in unison, as if they were sharing a lament about something that was about to end.

"But they are returning today," Clodomiro said, looking down the dusty road that led to the village. His tone was like that of a man who knows the executioner is on his way. "And not only that, Bartolo. They are coming back changed, transformed, full of new ideas about love, service, forgiveness…"

*Bartolo*He made a gesture of annoyance, almost indignation.

—Oh no! I've been through that before. The last time Sufrida went to one of those congresses, she came back saying that she had to be like Mary, from the Bible. That I should also be a better "bearer of God." Can you imagine, Clodomiro? I barely carry a shopping bag and I already arrive with a sore back!

Clodomiro burst out laughing, but not from a lack of understanding.

—And that's not all. Do you remember the time when La Perfecta came back from the retreat of "dedicated wives"? She said that our marriage should be based on "dialogue" and "shared goals." Dialogue,

Bartolo! I got married to have peace, not to become a philosopher.

—But, my friend, don't you think there's something good about them coming back with those ideas? —Bartolo asked, more out of curiosity than conviction. —At least they don't come back bored, right? Clodomiro looked at him with half-closed eyes, as if Bartolo had suggested they give up coffee for coconut water.

—Well, yes, but those ideas always come with tasks for us. Because in the end, the one who ends up being "transformed" is the one. Whether to help more around the house, to be more attentive, to listen more… Bartolo scratched his chin and nodded slowly.

—You're right. Look, Sufrida always tells me that relationships are like wine: they get better with time. But the last time she talked to me about it, I ended up washing the dishes to "contribute to the aging." The two of them burst out laughing, but soon fell silent again, each lost in their own thoughts.

"So what do we do?" Clodomiro asked finally. "We can't just accept them as if nothing happened. They're going to spill all their thoughts on us and look at us with those eyes that say, 'This man doesn't understand anything about spiritual life.'"

"We have to be prepared," Bartolo replied in an almost military tone. "Look, when Sufrida arrives, I'll listen to her for a while, tell her that everything sounds very interesting, and then I'll make her some coffee. That always distracts her."

"What if it doesn't work?" Clodomiro asked, worried.

—So I move on to plan B: I tell him that I've been thinking about it too. I make up something about how I realized I need to be more patient or something. They love to hear that one is "in process." Clodomiro looked at him with admiration.

—You are a genius, Bartolo. I will do the same, but I will add that while I was alone, I thought a lot about everything Perfecta does for me. That always moves her. The sound of an engine interrupted their conversation. It was the bus that was coming from the Marian congress. Bartolo and Clodomiro jumped up, like two soldiers ready for battle.

"Here they come," said Clodomiro, swallowing.

The bus stopped and several women got out, talking animatedly. Suffering and Perfect were among them, their faces beaming and their enthusiasm seeming to fill the air.

"Clodomiro!" Perfecta shouted, running towards him with open arms.

"Bartolo!" Sufrida exclaimed, with a smile that mixed love and expectation.

The two men exchanged a quick glance, as if to say, "God bless us." But before they could execute their plans, their wives began to speak.

—Clodomiro, I've been thinking about you a lot these days... —said Perfecta, taking his hands.

—Bartolo, you don't know how much I appreciate everything you do for me... —said Sufrida, looking him in the eyes with unusual sincerity.

The two men stood frozen, confused by this unexpected turn of events. They had expected lectures and long reflections, but instead they were receiving something they didn't know how to handle: gratitude.

That evening, as they helped with dinner and listened to stories from the Congress, Bartolo and Clodomiro looked at each other across the table, each with a resigned smile. Maybe it wouldn't be so bad, they thought. After all, if there was one thing they had learned from their wives, it was that life always had its surprises, and that even martyrs could find solace in love. However, the Marian Congress had not ended and they had to go to a nearby place for the last conference. Their husbands were happy because at least one day they would be without them.

A path to transformation

In a modest but welcoming room, illuminated by the soft rays of an afternoon that seemed to want to stay, the four women met after the conference, each with her story, her burdens and her own vision of life. It was no coincidence that they were there, although none of them had planned it as something transcendental. It had been an invitation, almost fortuitous, to a conference on the Virgin Mary. What none of them imagined was that that afternoon would become a turning point. Sufrida arrived at the place carrying not only a heavy bag, but a life full of sacrifices that never seemed to be enough. Her face reflected the wear and tear of so many responsibilities that had fallen on her shoulders since she was young. Mother of four children, she had dedicated every moment to ensuring that they lacked nothing, completely forgetting about herself. Her motto was: "Life is difficult, but you have to keep going." When the speaker spoke about Mary at the foot of the cross, Sufrida felt a pang in her heart. She imagined herself, carrying not only her own crosses, but those of her family, her friends, and even those of strangers who always came to her. But the speaker said something that resonated like a deep echo: "Service is not only carrying, but also knowing how to remain. To remain in love, not in resentment. To remain in faith, not in complaint." Suffering, she closed her eyes. To remain. She had not remained. She had run, fought, struggled against life, but she had never remained. And for the first time in a long time, she thought that perhaps she could stop, breathe, and let God carry part of her cross. Perfecta was second in the row of chairs. Her hair, impeccably combed, and her outfit, perfectly coordinated, spoke of a life in which no mistakes were allowed. Her world was an agenda filled with schedules met to the second and tasks performed with excellence. From the outside, it seemed that she had everything under control, but inside, Perfecta lived with a constant fear of failing. When the speaker spoke of the Wedding at Cana, something snapped in Perfecta. Maria had seen a need that was not essential, but that represented the happiness of the bride and groom. "Service is not limited to what is necessary; the true measure of service is happiness," the speaker said, and the words echoed in her mind. Perfecta remembered the times she had refused to accompany her daughter to play, saying that she was busy with more important things. She remembered the nights when she had stayed up late correcting minute details on projects that no one else would notice. She realized that her perfection had created a wall between her and the people she loved. "Perhaps true service is not in the perfect, but in the happy," she thought, and she felt something new: the possibility of breaking free. She sat bent over in a chair at the back of the room,She was hunched over as if the weight of something invisible was pushing her to the ground. Her life had been a series of imposed decisions, of paths chosen by others. She had always accepted because saying no seemed selfish, but over time, her "yes" had lost all meaning. When the speaker spoke about the Visitation, he mentioned a phrase that made Doblada raise her head for the first time: "True service is born of love and freedom, not of obligation or guilt." Doblada felt that a door had opened. Mary was not forced to visit Elizabeth; she did it because she wanted to, because her heart was full. For the first time, Doblada wondered if her service was born of love or fear of rejection. The idea of being able to choose how and whom to serve seemed revolutionary to her. For the first time in a long time, she considered that her back could be straightened. Cáemebien, the last of the four, had arrived at the conference late, invited by a friend who insisted that "it would do her good." Always smiling and proud, Caemebien was the woman everyone wanted around because she made others feel better about themselves. But what few knew was that behind her laughter and jokes,

Caemebien struggled with an emptiness she couldn't fill. When the speaker talked about Pentecost, about how Mary was there without reprimanding the disciples for their mistakes, something in Caemebien changed. The speaker said, "Mary doesn't recriminate; she accepts, loves, and prays. Her service is not in pointing fingers, but in uniting." Caemebien thought about her relationships. Although she was "loved," she had built superficial connections, avoiding touching on deep or difficult subjects. She never wanted to make anyone uncomfortable, but that had made her relationships fragile and empty. She realized that true service involved facing discomfort to build something stronger.Caemebien was the woman everyone wanted around because she made others feel better about themselves. But what few knew was that behind her laughter and jokes, Caemebien struggled with an emptiness she couldn't fill. When the speaker talked about Pentecost, about how Mary was there without reprimanding the disciples for their mistakes, something in Caemebien changed. The speaker said, "Mary doesn't recriminate; she accepts, loves, and prays. Her service is not in pointing fingers, but in uniting." Caemebien thought about her relationships. Although she was "loved," she had built superficial connections, avoiding touching on deep or difficult subjects. She never wanted to make anyone uncomfortable, but that had made her relationships fragile and empty. She realized that true service involved facing discomfort to build something stronger.Caemebien was the woman everyone wanted around because she made others feel better about themselves. But what few knew was that behind her laughter and jokes, Caemebien struggled with an emptiness she couldn't fill. When the speaker talked about Pentecost, about how Mary was there without reprimanding the disciples for their mistakes, something in Caemebien changed. The speaker said, "Mary doesn't recriminate; she accepts, loves, and prays. Her service is not in pointing fingers, but in uniting." Caemebien thought about her relationships. Although she was "loved," she had built superficial connections, avoiding touching on deep or difficult subjects. She never wanted to make anyone uncomfortable, but that had made her relationships fragile and empty. She realized that true service involved facing discomfort to build something stronger.

The conference ended, but something had begun in those four women. In the silence that remained at the end, while others left, they remained in their seats. None of them said anything at first, but their eyes met, and in that instant they understood that something had changed in all of them. Sufrida was the first to speak.

—Do you think it's possible...? Is it really possible to let someone else carry some of what we're carrying?

*Perfect*He took her hand.

—I think so. Maybe it's not about having someone else do it, but about learning to let go. I... I've always wanted to do everything on my own, but today I realized that I need to learn to trust others.

Folded, with a trembling voice, he added:

—What if we start choosing? I mean, choosing where we put our time, our energy. Not to escape, but to make sense of it.

Fall in love with me, who had been listening until then, smiled.

—I think we've already started. The fact that we're here, talking about this, is a step. Maybe... maybe we can do it together.

That afternoon was not an end, but a beginning. The four women left the room with lighter hearts and one idea in mind: transforming their lives through service. Sufrida decided she would seek help to learn to delegate and rest. Perfecta committed to dedicating time to her family, even if it meant abandoning perfection. Doblada began to work on saying "no" without guilt, choosing the causes in which she could truly put her love. And Cáemebien set out to deepen their relationships, seeking truth and not just comfort. The path would not be easy, but something in them had changed. Like Mary, they began to see service not as a burden, but as a gift; not as a sacrifice that empties, but as a love that fills. In their own lives, they began to carry God's blessing, becoming, each in their own way, bearers of his love. And so, the conference that had begun as just another event in their schedules, became the beginning of a new way of living, loving and serving.

A New Dawn:
The Transformation of
Suffering and Perfect

The bell tower of the village church rang out with a soft, slow ringing. The Marian congress had concluded, and the small town seemed to breathe more calmly. It was not just the fresh evening air that brought a new scent of hope, but something much deeper: the change in the hearts of the women who had participated in the retreat. Suffering and Perfecta returned home with a renewed light in their eyes, one that their husbands, Bartolo and Clodomiro, would soon notice.

The conferences on Mary had not only been a space for prayer and reflection, but a meeting of stories, of shared pains that were transformed into hope. It was there that they met Doblada and Cáemebien, two women whose lives had been marked by even deeper tragedies. Doblada, with her slow walk and a sadness that seemed to have nested in her soul, had shared her story. It was toxic but she had lived a very painful experience. She had lost her only son in an accident and, since then, she felt that life had bent her like a tree after a storm. However, when she heard the teachings about Mary at the foot of the cross, she found comfort. The Virgin had not only lost her Son; she had given him up out of love. In that surrender, Doblada discovered a purpose: to transform her pain into service to others.

Please feel free to contact me, On the other hand, she carried her sadness differently. She always smiled, even when she told her story: a marriage that had collapsed from abuse and indifference. But her encounter with Mary, the woman of Pentecost who united the apostles in prayer, showed her that even in chaos, faith could rebuild what was broken. "We fall," she said, "but we always get up because God never stops holding us up."

These stories touched Sufrida and Perfecta deeply. Sufrida, accustomed to carrying the complaints and frustrations of her daily life, recognized herself in Doblada. "I too have let myself be bent," she thought, "but perhaps I have not known how to give my burdens to the Lord as she is learning."

Perfect, always obsessed with making everything impeccable, from her home to her image in front of others, felt reflected in Cáemebien. "Maybe my search for perfection has been a way of hiding my insecurities," she mused, "but I can be perfect in

another way: by loving more and demanding less."
Upon returning home, the two women were
determined to change. They sat together in the town
square before seeing their husbands, while the last
rays of the sun dyed the horizon gold.

"What are you going to tell Bartolo?" asked
Perfecta, adjusting her shawl over her shoulders.

—I have been a martyr in my head, but not in my
heart —Suffering replied with a soft smile—. I no
longer want to complain. If Mary could give her life
to loving service, why can't I do it too?

Perfecta nodded, looking at the bell tower.

—I'm going to tell Clodomiro that I don't want to
keep looking for faults in him. I want to build with
him, not control everything.

When they both arrived home, Bartolo and
Clodomiro were already waiting for them. They had
not been oblivious to the days of reflection about
Maria; they had enjoyed them, yes, but they had also
realized how much they depended on them, although
they would never admit it out loud. Bartolo, with his
good-natured demeanor, pretended to be busy
sanding a bench in the yard when Sufrida came in.
She approached, looked at him tenderly, and took the
sandpaper from his hands.

—Bartolo, leave that for a moment. We need to talk.

He looked at her, surprised by the softness in her voice.

"Are you back with your things from the retreat?" he joked, trying to lighten the moment.

—Yes, but not like you think —she answered, taking a seat beside him—. I have realized that I have been living with resentments that you do not deserve. I have carried them as if they were yours, but they are not. I want to change. Bartolo did not know what to say. Sufrida had not looked at him like that for years. For the first time, he saw her with a peace that was strange, but comforting.

Next door, Perfecta had found Clodomiro reading the newspaper on the sofa. He looked up, a little defensively, as if he were expecting a sermon.

"Clodomiro," said Perfecta, sitting down opposite him, "I was wrong." That made him put down the paper completely.

—What do you mean, wrong?

—I've been obsessed with everything being perfect. With you, with the house, with our life. But

I've understood that love isn't in the details that I try to control, but in learning to let you be who you are.

*Clodomiro*He opened his mouth, then closed it. Finally, he said:

—Well, that... I didn't expect that.

That evening, the two couples dined together at Bartolo's house. Sufrida and Perfecta shared their experiences, the stories of Doblada and Cáemebien, and the lessons they had learned from the Virgin Mary. Bartolo and Clodomiro listened attentively, perhaps for the first time in a long time.

"So there won't be so much drama anymore?" Bartolo asked at last, raising an eyebrow cautiously.

"We don't promise perfection," Sufrida replied, winking. "But we do promise a lot of love."

—And fewer complaints —Perfecta added, laughing.

*Bartolo*and Clodomiro exchanged glances. There was hope on the horizon, but the most important thing was that, for the first time, everyone seemed ready to walk together towards a new beginning. In the heart of the town, under the stars that lit up the sky, the transformation had begun.

The bingo of hope

In the quiet but peculiar neighborhood of San Gregorio, the streets were beginning to whisper stories of transformation. The protagonists of this change were Sufrida and Perfecta, who, after the Marian congress, had decided not only to change their own lives, but also to impact those of their neighbors. Inspired by the example of the Virgin Mary, they set themselves an ambitious mission: to take Quedirán, Poco-me-importa, Rigoroso and Fructuoso to a conference entitled "Mary and Eve: two women, two paths." The first obstacle was clear: none of their neighbors wanted to go.

"A lecture? From Maria and Eve?" Quedirán snorted as he adjusted his hair in front of the living room mirror. "What people say is that you're wasting your time. What are they going to think if they see me there?" I-don't-care, hunched over in a plastic chair on his porch, barely looking up from his phone.

—I don't know, I'm not interested. Rigorous, with his severe expression, he crossed his arms.

—And why would I go? That conference is not going to change my life.

Finally, Fructuoso, the Youtuber, burst out laughing while reviewing his comments on social media.

—Sure, sure, let me go! I'll record some clips for my followers, play something motivational, and that's it. But, girls, fifty dollars is a lot to listen to old stories.

*Suffered*and Perfecta did not give up. After hearing all these excuses, they came up with a plan. They decided to organize a bingo to raise the 200 dollars needed to cover the cost of their neighbors' tickets. "If they don't want to go out of their own free will, let them go out of gratitude," said Perfecta with determination.

Bingo: more than just a game

On bingo night, the San Gregorio community hall was filled with laughter, excited shouts, and the irresistible aroma of freshly baked empanadas. Sufrida and Perfecta had spent hours decorating the place with white and blue balloons, the colors of the Virgin Mary.

—Bingo, top right corner, prize: basket of fresh fruit —Sufrida announced enthusiastically from the microphone.

*They will remain*He showed up at the end of the night, not to play, but to make sure his appearance was impeccable for any audience present. Rigorous, although he grumbled at first, ended up participating because "the rules were clear," and he couldn't resist the chance to win. I-don't-care arrived, as always, without much enthusiasm, but seeing that the food was free, he decided to stay. Fructuoso even recorded a live broadcast, presenting himself as the patron of the event, although he hadn't contributed a single cent.

At the end of the night, Sufrida and Perfecta managed to raise the money needed for the tickets. With the enthusiasm of a well-deserved victory, they went to their neighbors.

The surprise of the gift

"They'll say, Rigorous, I-don't-care, Fructuoso," Perfecta announced the next day as she knocked on each one's door. "We have a surprise."

"What kind of surprise?" Quediran asked, raising an eyebrow as he inspected his nails.

"They're going to the conference on Mary and Eve," Sufrida said, handing out an envelope with the tickets.

"Are we paying?" Perfecta interrupted, anticipating any excuse. "No. We have raised the money so that you can attend."

The disbelief was collective. I-don't-care did not even hide his astonishment.

—Did they spend money on us?

Rigorously he crossed his arms.

—I can't accept something I haven't earned.

"Oh, come on, Rigorous," Fructuoso interrupted, looking at his ticket with interest. "You don't look a gift horse in the mouth, do you?"

In the end, amidst looks of bewilderment and curiosity, everyone accepted.

The conference: two women, two paths

The day of the conference arrived. Quediran wore an impeccable suit and his best perfume, making sure no one would mistake him for a devotee. I-don't-care-anymore was in jeans and a T-shirt, with the expression of someone who wanted to be anywhere else. Rigoroso took notes during the introduction, looking for inconsistencies in the speech. Fructuoso, of course, broadcast live from the auditorium, making sure his followers saw how "dedicated" he was.

However, something unexpected happened. The depth of the speaker's words, comparing Mary's courageous "yes" to Eve's defiant "no," began to pierce through the layers of superficiality, indifference, rigidity and convenience in each of them.

*They will remain*He felt that the obsession with his appearance was hiding an insecurity he had never faced. I-don't-care, for the first time, thought that maybe it was worth worrying about something other than his comfort. Rigorous found himself moved by Maria's example of forgiveness, unable to ignore the possibility that his inflexibility was alienating him from others. And Fructuoso, though still broadcasting, began to reflect on how much hypocrisy there was in his motivational messages.

Back in San Gregorio, the group of neighbors was unusually quiet. Something had changed in them, although not all of them would admit it right away.

"Well, it was interesting," Quediran murmured, looking at Suffering and Perfect with a restrained smile. "Perhaps there is something more to learn."

"It wasn't so bad," I-don't-care added with a shrug. "Maybe… I'll sign up for another event."

Rigorous, always stern, nodded.

—The teachings have merit. We need to reflect more.

*Fruitful*He took off his headphones and, for the first time, did not try to record anything.

—Thanks for insisting. Maybe I need to practice what I preach.

*Suffered*and Perfecta looked at each other and smiled. The seed had been planted. In the heart of the neighborhood, a transformation was beginning to germinate, one that, with faith and patience, could blossom into something beautiful and lasting.

At the conference, Perfecta had taken her notes and wanted to meet in the village's community hall to explain and clarify what the speaker had said, so they invited everyone from the village to reflect on the figure of the Virgin Mary. Perfecta would lead the event.

Mary and Eve:
two women, two paths

The small community hall of San Gregorio was full of murmurs and expectations. It was the first time that Perfecta, always known for her haughty character and her tendency to avoid crowds, had decided to share what she had learned at the conference with her neighbors. At her side, Sufrida encouraged her with a smile, holding in her hands a small notebook with the notes they had both taken.

"You're ready," Sufrida said, squeezing her hand. "They need to hear this."

Perfecta nodded, taking a deep breath before standing up. She had spent weeks reviewing her notes, memorizing the words and preparing herself not only to speak, but to touch the hearts of those willing to listen.

In front of her, a heterogeneous audience looked at her with a mixture of curiosity and skepticism: Quedirán, with his eternal concern for appearances; Poco-me-importa, indifferent as always; Rigoroso, with his critical expression; and Fructuoso, who recorded everything with his camera, looking for content for his channel. There were also other neighbors from the neighborhood, men and women who had come because, if there was one thing they knew about Perfecta, it was that she never spoke without reason.

"Thank you for being here," Perfecta began, her voice warm but firm. "Today I want to share something that has changed my life, something I heard at the conference about Mary and Eve, two women who represent two opposite paths." The room fell silent. Even Little-I-Care stopped looking at his phone for a moment, intrigued by Perfecta's serious tone.

Eve's Way. Perfecta opened her notebook and read the first lines of her notes, looking up at her listeners.

—Eve was the first woman created by God, destined to be Adam's companion, to live in harmony in paradise. But Eve took a different path. When the wicked angel, the serpent, tempted her, she decided to follow her own judgment instead of obeying God.

Rigorous raised an eyebrow.

—And what about Adam? He also disobeyed.

"That is true," Perfecta replied calmly. "But Eve was the one who listened to the wrong voice, the one who took the first step towards disobedience. Standing beside the tree of good and evil, she fell into pride, believing that she could be like God. And in that act, she bore a fruit for death, a fruit that affected not only her, but all of humanity."

The silence in the room was palpable. Even Fructuoso had lowered his camera, attentive to Perfecta's words.

—Eve not only fell, but she pushed Adam into rebellion. And from that broken union with God came sin, death, and the first murderer, Cain, her own son. Eve, who was created to be a source of life, became the mother of an act of death.

*They will remain*He looked uncomfortable, adjusting the collar of his shirt as if the words weighed him down. I-don't-care sighed, but said nothing.

The Way of Mary. Perfecta paused before continuing.

—But there is another woman, another story, another path. Mary, the mother of Jesus, represents obedience, humility and fidelity. Suffering's face lit up when she heard these words, as if she had been waiting for them all night.

—When the angel Gabriel visited Mary, he brought her a message that would change the history of humanity. Mary did not hesitate, she did not question, she did not let herself be carried away by pride. Her response was clear and simple: "Let it be done to me according to your word."

—Of course, because she was perfect, wasn't she? —Fructuoso murmured, without malice but with a certain skepticism.

*Perfect*She looked at him with an understanding smile.

—Not because she was perfect, but because she had faith. Mary was obedient even in the most difficult moments. On the tree of the cross, when her Son was being crucified, she remained faithful. She never stopped trusting in God, even in the midst of the greatest pain a mother can experience.

"What does that have to do with us?" asked a woman from the back.

Perfecta took a sip of water before answering.

—It has everything to do with us. Mary and Eve are examples of what should be done and what should not be done, but they are also witnesses. The question we must ask ourselves is: whose disciples are we?

Mary or Eve? What kind of woman/man am I: a source of life or a source of ruin?

*Perfect*He paused for a moment, letting his words echo through the room before continuing.

—Woman is the source of life, both physically and spiritually. But for that very reason, the devil attacks us. If a woman has God in her heart, she can pour out blessing, hope and love on her family, her community, and the world. But if she doesn't have God in her heart, she can become a channel of destruction.

*They will remain*He frowned, as if he were thinking for the first time in a long time. I-Care-Not crossed his arms, but his gaze showed interest. Even Rigorous, who had seemed critical at first, now seemed more receptive.

"We see it every day," Perfecta continued. "In our decisions, in how we treat others, in how we face temptations. Do we obey God, like Mary, or do we follow our own judgment, like Eve?"

Change is in our hands. Sufrida, who had remained silent until then, stood up to support her friend.

—We are not saying that it is easy. I myself have often followed Eve's path: pride, disobedience, believing that I can do everything on my own. But since I began to seek God, I have understood that only in Him do I find the strength to change.

—I can say the same thing —Perfecta added. — For a long time I thought I had to be perfect in everything, that I had to control every aspect of my life. But I have learned that perfection is not in me, but in God.

"And what do they expect from us?" asked Riguroso, with his typical serious expression.

"Just think about it," Perfecta replied. "We are not here to judge anyone, but to invite you to think about which path you are following. Mary and Eve are two paths, and the choice is in our hands."

That night, something changed in the San Gregorio neighborhood. Perfecta and Sufrida's words had planted a seed in the hearts of their neighbors. Quedirán, always concerned with appearances, began to wonder if his obsession with what others thought was keeping him from what really mattered. Little-I-care, for the first time, he became curious about something beyond his own indifference. Rigorous, though still critical, began to see the importance of forgiveness and humility. Even Fructuoso, the ever-brash Youtuber, lowered his camera and decided to listen carefully.

In the days that followed, Perfecta and Sufferida continued to share what they had learned, not just with words, but with actions. They organized meetings, helped those in need, and showed by their example that Mary's path was not easy, but it was full of blessing. And while not everyone in the neighborhood changed immediately, one thing was certain: the echo of that conference, of those words, would resonate in San Gregorio for a long time, reminding them that there are always two paths, and that the decision of which to follow is in our hands.

*Perfect*and Sufrida, still excited by the success of the event, met the next day in Perfecta's small living room. The walls, adorned with religious images and inspirational phrases, seemed to resonate with the same energy they had felt in the community hall the night before.

"Did you notice how many people came?" Sufrida asked, with a mixture of surprise and satisfaction.

"Not only that, Suffering," Perfecta replied, stirring a cup of tea. "Did you notice their faces? There was curiosity, interest… even in those who came more out of obligation than true conviction."

They were silent for a moment, letting the magnitude of what had happened sink into their

hearts. They had filled the hall, something they never imagined. But along with the satisfaction came a question they couldn't ignore.

"What now?" Suffering finally said, breaking the silence. Perfecta shrugged, putting the spoon aside.

—I don't know. What we did yesterday was good, but... is it enough?

As they reflected, echoes of the conversations they had heard after the event began to form in their minds. Many people had approached them to thank them, but also asked them questions.

"Did you notice what they said?" Sufrida asked, leaning forward. "Many mentioned the Virgin of Guadalupe and the Virgin of Fatima."

—Yes, and that caught my attention. Almost everyone considers themselves devout, but... — Perfecta hesitated for a moment before continuing—. What does it really mean to be devout?

*Suffered*He nodded, remembering how some of the attendees seemed to confuse devotion with simple rituals or inherited customs.

—That's true. And I also think that few people really know the context of her apparitions.

Guadalupe, Fatima... each one has a powerful message, but who understands it in depth?

The conversation took a clear direction. The previous event had been a success, but now they had a new challenge: to deepen the faith of their community, to help them understand what it meant to be truly devout and why the apparitions of the Virgin were much more than nice stories or spectacular miracles.

"What do you think about organizing another event?" Perfecta suggested, her eyes shining with determination. "Something dedicated to explaining what a devotion is and the meaning of the apparitions of Guadalupe and Fatima." Sufrida smiled, infected by her friend's enthusiasm.

—I love the idea. But this time, we're going to need to prepare even better. This isn't just about organizing a talk; it's a mission. Both women spent the rest of the afternoon planning. They searched for information, contacted people who could help them, and thought of ways to make the event accessible and attractive to everyone. They knew it wouldn't be easy, but they also knew that the impact could be transformative. So what had begun as a simple question—"What now?"—became the first step

toward a new adventure of faith and service. For Perfecta and Sufrida, the journey was just beginning.

Perfecta's conference: The Virgin of Guadalupe and her message of faith

The auditorium was packed. A reverent murmur ran through the room as Perfecta approached the microphone, her demeanor humble but confident. People knew her well; she was not only a devout woman, but also someone who had spent weeks preparing for this moment. She had read old books, consulted historical documents, and had even visited specialized libraries in search of details about the apparitions of the Virgin of Guadalupe. She had even met with priests and experts to ensure that her words carried the weight of truth and the rigor of research. Perfecta knew that she was not only speaking of faith, but also of history, culture, and miracles.

With a deep sigh, he prepared to begin. "Do you know how many times the Virgin of Guadalupe appeared?" he asked, letting silence envelop the room. "Before we answer, let's understand something important: the Church, when she invites us to believe, does not do so out of whim or fantasy. She does so based on facts, on realities that have been carefully verified. God is great and powerful, but he also asks

us for prudence and discernment. Today we are going to go through these apparitions together, not only with our hearts, but also with our minds."

First appearance: Saturday, December 9, 1531

*Perfect*He recounted how it all began on Mount Tepeyac, on a cold December morning. "Juan Diego, a simple man, a widower, about 55 years old, was climbing the hill as he usually did on his way to catechism. But that day would not be like any other. He heard birdsong, a sound so melodious that it seemed to come from heaven itself. Suddenly, a voice called out to him: 'Juan Dieguito, the most beloved.' It was a voice full of sweetness and tenderness."

Perfecta paused in her story for a moment to look at the audience. "Can you imagine? Juan Diego saw what he described as a little girl, but he soon understood that it was not just any little girl. The Virgin introduced herself as 'the perfect ever Virgin Mary, mother of the true God.' And she asked him something clear: 'I want a temple to be built here, to hear the cries and sorrows of my children, to purify their miseries and pains.'"

As she recounted this, Perfecta recalled how, during her research, she had found records about the exact location where this apparition occurred and the precise words that were etched into the collective memory. "Juan Diego, moved, went to Bishop Juan de Zumárraga, a wise but skeptical Franciscan. The bishop did not immediately believe him, which, as we will see, has a reason."

Second appearance: Saturday, December 9, in the afternoon

*Perfect*She continued. "Juan Diego returned to Tepeyac, full of doubts. He confessed to the Virgin that the bishop had not believed him. With humility, he asked her to send someone else, someone more important than him. But the Virgin, with her maternal love, encouraged him to persevere. She told him that he was her messenger, her chosen one."

*Perfect*He paused again, recalling his conversations with theologians. "It is important to understand the bishop's skepticism. It was not a lack of faith, but prudence. The Church, as St. Ignatius of Loyola teaches us, always carefully examines these phenomena to distinguish the divine from the human or even the evil. We must not forget that even the devil can disguise himself as an angel of light."

Third appearance: Sunday, December 10

"The next day, Juan Diego returned to Tepeyac after his second interview with the bishop. The latter had asked him for a sign, something to confirm the authenticity of the Virgin's message. The Virgin was not bothered by this request. On the contrary, she told Juan Diego to return the next day and that she would then give him the necessary proof."

*Perfect*He explained with emotion that this detail had been one of the most studied by historians. "The bishop was not seeking to contradict Juan Diego, but to follow the process that the Church has always respected: prudence, discernment and confirmation. The Virgin here showed her respect for the authority of the Church, something that she also teaches us."

Fourth apparition: Tuesday, December 12, early in the morning

"Juan Diego did not return on Monday as the Virgin had asked him to. But it was not because of disobedience, but because his uncle, Juan Bernardino, was seriously ill. Filled with charity, he decided to find a priest to administer the last sacraments to him. He went around the hill to avoid the Virgin, but She, who sees everything, came out to meet him."

*Perfect*He paused to emphasize this moment. "The Virgin was not offended. On the contrary, she said to him tenderly: 'Am I not here, I who am your mother? Your uncle has already been healed.' Then she asked him to go up to the mountain, where he would find flowers as a sign for the bishop. It was

December, a cold winter, and yet Juan Diego found fresh roses, a miracle in itself."

Fifth appearance: at the same time, with Juan Bernardino

*Perfect*She concluded the account of the apparitions. "While this was happening to Juan Diego, the Virgin also appeared to his uncle, Juan Bernardino, healed him and revealed her name to him: 'Saint Mary of Guadalupe'. This double miracle confirms that what is happening here can only come from God. The tilma, with its miraculous image, is the testimony that we all know today."

Final thoughts

*Perfect*He concluded his lecture with a call to faith and reason. "The Virgin of Guadalupe teaches us so many things: humility, obedience, charity, and above all, love for Christ and his Church. Her image is not only a miracle in itself, but also a visual catechesis that reminds us that the Gospel adapts to all cultures, but always leads us to the absolute truth that is Jesus Christ."

*Perfect*She had managed not only to transmit knowledge, but also to ignite faith in the hearts of those who listened to her. The conference concluded with a profound reflection on the teachings of the Virgin of Guadalupe. Perfecta listed seven key points:

The gospel transcends and purifies all cultures, putting Christ at its center.

Mary, prayerful, virgin and mother, whose image is a living catechesis.

Mary turns her back on the sun of the Aztecs, indicating that the true sun is Christ.

Mary leads us to Christ, always as an intercessor.

Obedience to the Church, respecting legitimate authorities.

Juan Diego's familiarity with the Virgin, marked by a relationship of tenderness and trust.

The promise of his loving presence, in words like: "Am I not here, I who am your Mother?"

*Perfect*He closed his speech with a serene smile, leaving a message that resonated in everyone's hearts:

—The Virgin of Guadalupe teaches us to live with faith, humility and obedience. She reminds us that, at every moment, Christ must be the center of our lives.

The auditorium erupted in applause as Sufrida took the stage to thank the attendees and remind them that the next lecture would be on devotions to Our

Lady of Fatima. The energy in the room was palpable; the message of Our Lady of Guadalupe had touched souls and ignited hearts. However, Perfecta is thinking of Sufrida. Perfecta, with her warm smile, approached Sufrida after the lecture. She had noticed her pensive expression throughout the presentation on Our Lady of Guadalupe. It was as if something inside her was struggling to find an outlet, as if the words about Juan Diego and Our Lady resonated in her own life. Perfecta, always attentive to the emotions of others, sensed that this was the moment to reach out a helping hand. "Sufrida, can I talk to you for a moment?" she asked in a tone full of empathy. Sufrida, surprised but grateful, nodded. Together they sat in a corner of the room, away from the bustle of the others. "I saw you were very attentive during the conference. It seems that the stories of the apparitions touched something inside you. Am I right?" Perfecta looked at her with sincere eyes, inviting her to open up. Sufrida sighed. "Yes, Perfecta. While you were talking, I couldn't stop thinking about Our Lady of Fatima. It is a devotion that has always caught my attention, but I have never dared to delve deeper into it. Maybe because I feel that, in my life, I have never been worthy of receiving divine consolation." Perfecta took Sufrida's hand tenderly. "Don't say that. Our Lady of Fatima's message is precisely for souls like yours, for those who carry suffering and struggles, but continue to walk with faith. It seems to me that you have a lot to contribute by reflecting on these apparitions. Why don't you try?" Sufrida looked at her doubtfully. "Me? What could I say that hasn't already been said?" "A lot," Perfecta answered without hesitation. "You have experienced pain, surrender, and sacrifice in ways that many could not imagine. This gives you a unique sensitivity to understand the message of Fatima: conversion, penance, and prayer. And I am sure that the Holy Spirit will guide you. Why don't you start by researching what happened to the three little shepherds? Read it with the eyes of your heart and write down your reflections. Then, we can share them together." Sufrida's face gradually brightened. Perfecta's proposal was not only a challenge, but also a balm for her wounded soul. She felt that, by reflecting on Our Lady of Fatima, she could also find answers for her own life. "Okay, I will do it. But I will need your help, Perfecta," she said with a slight smile. "I will always be here for you, Sufrida. Our Lady accompanies us both on this path." That day, the two women began a spiritual journey that would not only transform them, but also the lives of others.but also to those who would listen to the message that Sufrida would later share. The Virgin of Fatima, with her call

to love and conversion, would become a beacon of
hope for both of them.

Our Lady of Fatima: An encounter with faith and history

The day of the conference arrived after months of intense preparation. Sufrida had devoted weeks to deep and methodical study. In the libraries of her city she had examined historical documents, biographies of the shepherd children, and theological analyses of the apparitions. She had consulted with renowned priests and theologians, whose perspectives enriched her understanding. With the spiritual guidance of Perfecta, she had prayed fervently, asking for the light of the Holy Spirit to transmit the message of the Virgin with clarity and fidelity. As she entered the auditorium, Sufrida felt the weight of the moment. It was her opportunity to unite devotion with intellectual rigor, to show that faith and reason could dialogue fruitfully. Before an expectant audience, she began in a calm but passionate tone:

The Angel of Peace. "Before the apparitions of Our Lady in 1917, the shepherd children of Fatima - Lucia, Francisco and Jacinta - received visits from the Angel of Peace in 1916. These first manifestations were a spiritual preparation. The angel taught them to pray and to offer sacrifices for sinners. This divine pedagogy prepared their hearts for the great mission that Our Lady would entrust to them. It is important not to forget these first apparitions, since they remind us that prayer and sacrifice are the prelude to any significant divine intervention." To profitably understand the message of Fatima, it is necessary to understand the historical context.

The century of crisis. The 19th century had radically transformed Europe and the world. The Industrial Revolution changed not only the economy, but also the perception of the human being. Man was no longer the center; the machine displaced him. Children worked exhausting days, and the obsession with production dehumanized people. Human beings went from using tools to becoming an extension of them. At the same time, science, previously the domain of a few, became the arbiter of truth and progress. This "idolatry of science," as Leo XIII called it, displaced the Church as the moral and intellectual authority. In this environment, Karl Marx offered a radical response: scientific materialism and communism. Marx interpreted the exploitation of workers as a systemic problem and proposed a solution that supplanted the Christian message with a secular "redemption" based on class struggle.[9]".

Sufrida paused, letting the words sink in. "In the midst of this crisis of faith and humanity, Our Lady appears at Fatima. What makes her message so relevant? She calls us to return to the Gospel in 'dramatic hours of history.' However, it is crucial to avoid two common errors in the interpretation of Fatima:

The political interpretation: Many have reduced the apparitions to a response to communism, suggesting that Our Lady takes sides with a specific ideology. But her message is much deeper. It is not a response to Marx or a call to the extreme right. It is a call to conversion of heart, an invitation to all peoples and nations to live in the truth of the Gospel.

The esoteric interpretation: Others are obsessed with the 'secrets' of Fatima, speculating about conspiracies or hidden messages. This trivializes the message. Our Lady does not come to replace the Gospel with hidden enigmas, but to remind us that its essence is for everyone, not for a few initiates. The

---

[9]Cf. C. Altamira, The Marxisms of the New Century. Buenos Aires: Editorial Biblos, 2006.

true 'secret' of Fatima is the urgency of living the Gospel in its fullness.

Let us delve a little deeper into the knowledge of the Marxist idea to understand how important and current the message of Fatima is.

The industrial machinery roared in the factory, an unstoppable production gear that transformed meat into sausages, objects into surplus value, and human lives into accounting figures. Amidst this mechanical echo, the worker gave his strength, his health, and his time. He, a fundamental piece, supported capitalism while, paradoxically, receiving the minimum to survive. The rest—wealth, profit, property—flowed to the capitalist, the owner of the machines. This was the logic that Karl Marx tried to break down: a system where work generated wealth, but the worker remained excluded from it.[10].

Marx observed how surplus value, the additional value that products acquire when they are processed, became the cornerstone of capitalism. The example of the pig being turned into sausages illustrates the process: the capitalist invests in the animal, the

---

[10]Cf. A. Samuel, Marxism beyond Marx. Mexico: National Pedagogical University–Directorate of University Outreach and Diffusion–Editorial Promotion, 2004.

machine and the labour, but the fruit of that investment returns multiplied, not to the worker, but to the owner. While the capitalist accumulated machines and money, the worker accumulated children – offspring, his only wealth – perpetuating his role as a proletarian.

However, Marx's analysis was not limited to the economic. For him, this system was protected by a legal framework that ensured the privileges of the capitalist and the submission of the worker. The cycle continued, with the capitalist becoming more powerful, controlling not only the economy, but also the social superstructures: art, religion and education. Everything revolved around economic power.

In his historical vision, Marx perceived a constant struggle, a dialectic where the oppressed rebelled and took the place of the oppressor, perpetuating the cycle. To break this dynamic, his proposal was radical: the abolition of private ownership of the means of production. Only in this way, Marx imagined, could the advance of exploitation and hatred be stopped.

But that utopia turned into a dystopia. Communism, born as a response to injustice, degenerated into totalitarian systems. Marx's ideas flourished not in England, as he predicted, but in

Russia, where a regime was established that shot opponents, destroyed families and centralized the means of production in the hands of the state. A new elite emerged: the rulers, who perpetuated inequalities under a rhetoric of equality.

Marxism, in its quest to transform society, operated as a hate machine. It identified oppressed sectors—workers, peasants, women, sexual minorities—and mobilized them through indignation, encouraging marches and symbolic occupations. This model, according to Marxist logic, did not seek justice, but revenge. The engine that drove this machine was hatred: toward the oppressor, toward traditional institutions like the Church, and toward any value system that was not its own.

In a context of profound social unrest, the message of Fatima emerges with prophetic clarity: if humanity did not pray and convert, the errors of communism would spread throughout the world. But the problem, as the message points out, is not just economic. It is spiritual and moral. The real threat of communism lies not only in its failed economic proposition, but in its capacity to generate hatred and divide humanity. To counter this machinery of hatred, Fatima proposes three fronts:

Intellectual Front: Fight against scientism, the reduction of all truth to the realm of science, rescuing wisdom and testimony in preaching.

Social Front: Addressing the legitimate complaints of oppressed sectors, not from a place of hatred, but from a place of justice. The commitment must be to human dignity and the elimination of the causes of oppression.

Spiritual Front: Conversion, penance and prayer, as requested by the Virgin Mary.

Marx's legacy: A call to conversion. Marx was a preacher. His denunciation of economic injustices had an almost messianic tone, a call to the proletarians to rise up. However, his proposal, based on historical materialism and hatred as the engine of change, failed. But his machinery of hatred remains a threat, capable of infiltrating various areas of society.[11]

The relevance of the message of Fatima lies in its invitation to conversion. Only by disarming hatred with intelligence, justice and prayer will it be possible to build a truly human society, where the most forgotten are restored not as tools of revenge, but as

---

[11]Cf. M. Postone, Time, Labour and Social Domination: A Reinterpretation of Marx's Critical Theory. Madrid: Marcial Pons, 2006.

brothers and sisters in dignity. That is the message of Fatima.

"During the six apparitions of Our Lady in 1917, Lucia, Francisco and Jacinta received a message of prayer, penance and hope. Our Lady showed them visions of heaven, hell and purgatory, urging them to pray especially for sinners and to offer sacrifices for their conversion. At the fourth apparition, she taught them the recitation of the Rosary as a spiritual weapon against evil. Finally, the miracle of the sun, witnessed by thousands of people, confirmed the authenticity of her words."

"Today, more than a century later, the message of Fatima remains relevant. We live in a world marked by new forms of idolatry: technology, consumerism and relativism. Our Lady reminds us that true change does not come from human ideologies, but from a sincere conversion to the Gospel. Her message is not a substitute for the Bible, but an invitation to take it seriously in the midst of the crises of our time."

Sufrida ended her talk with a personal invitation: "Our Lady calls each one of us. No matter how small or insignificant we feel, we can all be instruments of her message. Just as the little shepherds transformed the world with their fidelity, so can we. Let us pray, do penance and live the Gospel with courage. The message of Fatima is not just for theologians or historians; it is for you and me, here and now."

When she finished, the audience erupted in applause. Suffering, her eyes shining, she felt she had fulfilled her mission. She had not only shared Our Lady's message; she had embodied it, showing that even the most wounded heart can become a channel of grace and hope.

The Yes that Transforms: Stories of Faith and Change

Dusk was falling over the village, and in the small church, a group of neighbours gathered in silence after mass. The image of the Virgin under the title of Guadalupe and Fatima seemed to look at them with that serene expression of someone who understands human struggles but also the hopes that sustain them.

They will remain, Always caught in the chains of other people's opinions, he had dared to raise his eyes to Our Lady. Now he tried hard to free himself from the judgments of others, although it was difficult every day. Sometimes he fell back into his old habits, but he had begun to listen to an inner voice that was more powerful than the external voices. He regretted the quarrels and scandals in which he had been involved.

I-don't-care-much, Instead, she no longer responded with indifference and sarcasm. Little by little, her heart was opening, finding joy in small gestures of generosity towards others. Her neighbor Suffering, that woman with a face marked by the weight of years of work and pain, had decided to continue trusting. She had learned to give thanks even for the darkest nights, knowing that the light always comes, even if it is slowly.

Folded, With her bipolar diagnosis, she faced days of emotional ups and downs, but she relied on devotion to stay on track. She had stopped blaming her ex-boyfriends for her past and, although she still saw some as scapegoats, that resentment was beginning to fade. In its place, a genuine desire to move forward emerged.

Rigorous and Perfect, Those who had always cultivated appearances found themselves caught in the contradiction of admiring the changes in others and, at the same time, fearing the challenge of looking within. They found it more difficult, perhaps because they knew that true change would involve abandoning the mask they had lived with for so long.

For their part, Clodomiro and Bartolo remained, with a mixture of skepticism and astonishment at the change their wives were showing. "Let's see if this lasts," they said in murmurs, but even their hardened hearts were beginning to sense something new in their homes: peace. A peace they had perhaps never known before.

The entire town was changing, although the pace was not the same for everyone. However, at the heart of their individual transformations, the question resonated strongly: "What does it mean to be devoted to Our Lady?" It was not just praying novenas or carrying a holy card in one's pocket. It was something deeper: a constant openness to the will of God, a commitment to love beyond one's own strength, to forgive until one's heart stops bleeding, to look at others with mercy even when they do not deserve it. Being devoted to Our Lady meant trusting, as she did, in a divine plan that surpasses all understanding.

And you, reader, who have followed these stories up to this point, how does your faith influence your life? Have you asked yourself what devotion to the Virgin, under any invocation, means to you? How does it benefit you or what does it demand of you?

The characters in this story are still in the process. Some, like Doblada and Sufrida, are already taking firm steps towards a renewed life. Others, like Quedirán and Riguroso, are still fighting their own ghosts. But all of them, without exception, have the same opportunity as you: to let themselves be transformed by the love of God, by the example of Mary, and by a faith that does not stop at words but is translated into concrete actions. Life does not change overnight, but it changes when we say "yes" like Mary. A "yes" to patience with others, to reconciliation with our past, and to hope for a better future. Let us hope that the lives of these characters change. But, beyond them, the question remains: and you? Will you allow your life to change too?

www.ingramcontent.com/pod-product-compliance
Lightning Source LLC
Chambersburg PA
CBHW061320120726
48001CB00002B/604